DOTCOMBO & THE SURF_ACES

Internet Protectors & Adventurers

David Sharp

UPFRONT PUBLISHING
LEICESTERSHIRE

DOTCOMBO & THE SURF_ACES
Internet Protectors & Adventurers
Copyright © David Sharp 2003

ISBN 1-84426-227-8

First Published 2003 by
UPFRONT PUBLISHING
Leicestershire

DOTCOMBO & THE
SURF_ACES
Internet Protectors & Adventurers

This book is dedicated to Rebecca and Rachel.
My thanks to Robbie for his help with the illustrations.

About The Author

David Sharp was born in the town of Greenock, situated on the West Coast of Scotland in 1946, and has lived in West Kilbride, a small farming village thirty miles south of Greenock, since the early 1970s.

He worked at IBM for almost 28 years, during which time in the late 1980s, he spent almost four years living and working in Paris. He currently works for a European IT company as a business development manager.

He is married to Maureen and they have two grandchildren, Rebecca and Rachel, to whom this book is dedicated.

Football, all kinds of music and walking the dog are amongst his pastimes. He always wanted to be a writer, though other priorities got in the way!

He began the concept draft for this book in 1997 and developed it throughout 1998 and 1999. Working in his spare time he scribbled ideas, story lines, situations and characters in a pocket book whilst sitting in airplanes, airport waiting lounges and wherever the opportunity or inspiration occurred.

He is relieved to have finished this book after so many edits and rewrites and is now busily working through the second and third book in the series.

CONTENTS

THE ADVENTURE BEGINS

DotCombo sat back in her chair concentrating on the giant control panel in front of her; all seemed well. She swung around and gazed at the Multiwall, hundreds of screens showed business as usual with no apparent threats or problems.

She stood up, walked towards the huge windows that surrounded her central control module and looked out upon the most fantastic, magical and magnificent of views.

This vantage point put DotCombo right at the very centre, the heart, the pulse of the internet web could see the entire internet as it stretched from north to south and east to west in front of her. It was a huge blanket and it covered the whole of her vision at every angle.

As she walked round the circular module she could see thousands of e-mails working their way through the internet, passing the routing junctions as they made their way to their end-user addresses like little electrical charges weaving their way to their destinations. Files, documents and images cascaded across the internet in a similar fashion. Hits rained down on the numerous web sites, which DotCombo provided and protected. It was a vast tapestry of movement and colour. Each web site has its own colour coding and in a way it was this, which gave the internet its unusual visual dynamics. It was like an immense city, full of light, movement, colour, noise and excitement.

DotCombo was always amazed at the life the internet had; a life of its own, a life created by the millions of PC users who by the second accessed the system and surfed the web. It was growing daily and for this reason DotCombo considered her role managing the internet and ensuring its safety and security to be extremely important and increasing in importance as each new internet day passed. She took another look at the internet and once again returned to her chair behind the giant central control module.

Click, her operative and trainee Surf_Ace was responsible for operating the console and ensuring that everything was working properly. DotCombo didn't like surprises, nor did she welcome equipment failure at any time. She was relaxed now and eagerly awaited the arrival of Scanner and, most of all, the Surf_Aces.

The daily meeting between DotCombo and the Surf_Aces would start shortly. Scanner had prepared an overview, which he would use to brief the group on the current situations and incidents out on the internet.

DotCombo had some web time to reflect and she settled back in her chair, thinking.

It had been just over a web year now since her appointment and, barring a few unplanned activities, everything had seemed to go well. She had been congratulated by the Global Internet Zonal Management Alliance (GIZMA) on her disciplined approach and control. An added bonus were the Surf_Aces who had been an excellent addition to the internet protection team. DotCombo really did have the most important job of all and it was immediately visible if the internet didn't operate smoothly if security and safety issues occurred.

Her mind drifted to times gone by, she mused about her role, and the various individuals involved through the internet years good and bad.

How had she come to be in such an important position?

It all started for DotCombo with the advent of the internet and the World Wide Web. The internet is a global communications medium, which enables computer users, to interact with each other using e-mails, notes and messages, information files and data covering a wide and unlimited range of subjects. The internet also allows individuals and companies to create web sites, which are basically advertising and/or information vehicles for their products and services. At its best it's a simple but extremely modern computer-based fountain of information and knowledge which, with a telephone link, can be accessed by anyone.

Information of all kinds flows through the internet from end-user to end-user. Web sites are created, thousands of them every day, by individuals, small organisations, medium to large companies and the 'blue chip' corporations trading on the world stock exchanges, including the major banking and insurance companies.

At times sensitive data and information is resident in the web. Security is good, but immature, and active methods are being sought to protect the data, the information flow and the overall well-being of the system.

In the future almost all business transactions will be handled through the internet like direct online purchasing using credit cards which will be an everyday occurrence for all users. Already several companies offer and operate direct services. Anyone with access to a web site can order food, insurance, cars and much more. Users can browse through virtual supermarkets and buy the weekly shopping which will be delivered direct to their home address. It is possible to survive without leaving home, well almost; fresh air isn't available over the internet!

More and more people are working from home, as the ability to communicate and converse with end-users across the planet becomes commonplace.

As more and more users are attracted to the internet the opportunity for abuse, misinformation and corruption is significant and it will get worse. Lost or corrupt data and computer hacking will be prevalent as the potential for making large amounts of money through unscrupulous means attracts not only minor criminals but also major criminal organisations. The internet will need protecting and this task has been given to the world's number one information protector, enforcement officer and crime fighter: Dorothy T Combo, affectionately known as DotCombo, and her twenty-first century associates the Surf_Aces.

DotCombo is a highly intelligent, experienced, strong-willed, forceful, modern woman in every respect. She lives and breathes the security and well-being of the internet. DotCombo lives and manages her operation from the very heart of the internet. She is a natural leader and in this powerful role commands great respect throughout the internet industry and the millions upon millions of end-users. DotCombo was chosen for her experience, unlimited skills and a savage inbuilt mean streak!

Her central control module, located at the very heart of the internet, is the management centre and routing control point for all incoming/outgoing e-mails, documents, information, text, files and web site management. Her protection of these extends to all end-users who use the internet, large and small, there are no exceptions.

She processes the hits being made on each web site, updates web sites with new information and keeps them safe and secure. DotCombo guards and controls all the information that is stored on an unlimited number of magnetic Disks, called Information Disks.

The Information Disks are connected at random intervals to the Superhighway. The Superhighway is connected to and is the direct route into and out of the internet. All information being transferred to and from end-users, into and out of the internet, is visible to

DotCombo. Everything, and that really does mean everything, moving or transferring through the internet is managed and protected by DotCombo and her associates, the Surf_Aces.

What a job! she thought, *best job I have ever had – and the Surf_Aces, what a team*!

The Surf_Aces are a group of specialist internet protectors and crime fighters. Carefully chosen by DotCombo for their abilities, they have abundant energy, are extremely funny, enjoy their work and are totally fearless.

The Surf_Aces are expert surfers who surf around the internet seeking out and eliminating danger, their job is to attack anyone or anything that is likely to cause the internet to be destroyed or involve any information being lost, stolen or deleted. The Surf_Aces. ride on specially designed magnetic surfboards and occasionally will use unique foot discs. They can glide, hover and skim above the surface of the Information Disks, the Superhighway and around the internet. They have scanners fitted to their magnetic surfboards and foot discs that allow them to read information on the tracks of each Disk. If they are on patrol or on a special mission, by reading the data in each track they can if they choose infiltrate into the content of the Disk. This allows them to physically explore the Disk and make sure that it is working properly, it's not under attack or in danger. It also allows them to have fun and play in the Disks!

The Surf_Aces have on their magnetic surfboard a

waist-high panel and a detachable handheld pod which has laser sensors and direction finders which, once locked on, can direct them into the Disks. They can glide between the tracks on the Disks, this allows them to surf into a huge variety of situations, environments, worlds, games and adventures as they patrol the internet or as they seek, chase and locate their chosen target.

The Surf_Aces can surf very fast and it has been known for them to reach speeds of upwards of eight quantum calamities or more, five quantum calamities being the norm. Quantum calamities is the speed level programmed by DotCombo into the magnetic surfboards or foot discs used by the Surf_Aces. One quantum calamity is the equivalent of '300 kilometres per hour' earth speed.

Each Surf_Ace has on their handheld pod a retractable flat round device which they use to fire, blast, zap digital laser beams at their prey, or anyone or anything attacking them. The digital laser beam device is known to the Surf_Aces as their DBM. The DBM can be used as a handheld blaster and when not in use is attached by a magnetic force to a Mobile Command Belt (MCB) which they clip on to their waist.

There are four main Surf_Aces, three males and one female. They have trained together and worked as a unit for almost five web years and know each other's strengths and weaknesses. At her special request, they joined DotCombo on her appointment.

Each Surf_Ace is different, and although they

trained together their individual specialist skills and good team disciplines have been honed through extensive training and field experience.

The Surf_Aces live in the Information Data Bank, which is the holding zone for thousands of Disks not in use or not connected to the Superhighway at any given time. They have a state-of-the-art apartment located in the penthouse, which contains a huge control module similar to DotCombo's central control operation.

Discs from the Information Data Bank are sometimes released onto the Superhighway at DotCombo's command. Discs are released regularly using a Software Surfing Selection System, called '4S' that DotCombo created, designed, and is operated from her central control module at the heart of the internet.

Sometimes Disks are released to add new dimensions, downloads updated or revised information, create interest, introduce variety, update web sites, create new web sites, announce new ideas, and disperse virus protection tools and to outwit and stay ahead of those who plan an attack on the Disks and the internet.

DotCombo could not secure the internet and provide a basic level of protection without the Surf_Aces. It would be very dangerous to operate the internet, not only to hold Disks on the Superhighway but also in the Information Data Bank. Also the data being transferred around the internet at any particular moment could be at great risk if the Surf_Aces were not key members of her staff.

Like DotCombo, the Surf_Aces started with GIZMA as trainee support operatives. Their tasks were mainly administrative involving specific work assignments.

As the internet grew it was clear that a highly trained protection team was required to provide security for the internet and to the end-users. The role of the Surf_Aces was devised and conceived by Cache Downloader who worked for GIZMA at the time. The present group of Surf_Aces were chosen after a series of induction courses and special training exercises. They were also assessed for their intelligence levels in a very difficult and exacting IQ test. During their basic training the Surf_Aces spent several months with the crack divisions of the US and British armies. Each Surf_Ace has a code name to protect their true identity for security reasons.

Number one Surf_Ace is Refresh. He is an expert in disguise, is the most experienced Surf_Ace and is very clever, strong, brave and fearless. He will not hesitate to attack anything he considers is a threat to the internet, he is the unelected but respected leader of the Surf_Aces.

Number two Surf_Ace is Icon, the trendiest. An Afro-American, he is hip, always best dressed, sets new styles, sings a lot, is a talented musician who can play a variety of instruments. Icon's the most likely to get into and out of trouble, he's very talented and the perfect foil for Refresh – they work well together.

Number three Surf_Ace is Tooltip, the ideas and gadgets man. He's extremely funny, always smiling, happy, a natural joker and is excellent if the Surf_Aces are in a tight spot or extreme danger as he produces on-the-spot solutions or invents unique escape methods and appliances.

Last but by no means least is Media. She is athletic, clever and cute with a dark complexion and a sensational hairstyle. Media's probably the best surfer, but very bossy. If pushed she will champion Refresh as her favourite Surf_Ace. All the Surf_Aces keep a careful watch on Media and protect her, although she's more than capable of looking after herself and all of the others.

The Surf_Aces are always prepared and ready to act on every request and instruction given by DotCombo, they are her means of ensuring the internet is safe and secure. DotCombo also has two other accomplices who help her manage the smooth running of the internet.

Shortcut (his code name) is DotCombo's central control operative and trainee Surf_Ace. He's called Click by everyone due to the various clicking noises, like a computer mouse, he makes as he scurries about flicking buttons and clicking switches on the central control module. Click manages the communications. At DotCombo's request it will be Click that will send for her Surf_Aces or seek them out if she needs them urgently. A double click and he's off! Click operates the central control module for DotCombo unless she is personally in attack or battle mode, then she assumes full control of operations.

Scanner is a magnetic robot, a browser engine, whose job is to search for danger on the web, develop intelligence, prepare briefings and alert DotCombo and the Surf_Aces. He is tall and thin with a scanning head and a separate voice speaker unit. Scanner has a computer located in his midriff that he uses to interpret the information received from his scanning head.

Scanner provides important information and is expected to be aware of and up to date on all activity that may cause danger to the Disks and the internet.

DotCombo knew she had a good handpicked group and that – the confidence the end-users had – the future growth and the very existence of the internet would be secured, in fact almost guaranteed, by this elite team.

What a team, thought DotCombo, *the best in the business. I couldn't have handpicked them better!*

They knew they had to be.

In the early days there weren't many problems or trouble, data was lost here and there, but with so few end-users it could always be recovered quickly and with the minimum of fuss. Now though it was different. As the internet grew, more and more information passed through the system and end-users developed PC skills. It was now a real target and as such an entirely new and deadly enemy was on the loose, a real menace.

The menace was Ram Router and the Bugs, internet enemy par excellence. In the recent past DotCombo operated as a personal assistant to Ram Router who was in charge of the internet before DotCombo took over.

DotCombo smiled, she couldn't think about Ram without remembering some of his escapades. If it wasn't for the serious nature of their attacks and the resultant danger to the internet it might just be really funny.

She frowned as she gazed at the Multiwall, there was still no sign of anything happening and her mind returned again to times gone by.

Dorothy T Combo, or DotCombo as she was affectionately known throughout the internet, had come a long way from her humble beginnings.

She'd some military service behind her as a conscript and saw limited action in the Gulf War way back in the early 1990s, which she described as having 'rescued a few stricken airmen'. DotCombo smiled at the memory. She hadn't really planned her present career, in fact if anything it was fate, well maybe circumstances.

It's strange to think about it but if Ram Router hadn't been so stupid, I'd have married him and probably there'd be four or five little Ram clones by now! she thought. Instead Ram was now gone and DotCombo was in arguably the most important job in the modern world and Ram now her adversary.

Times have changed indeed, she thought.

She looked down at the central control module where Click sat working, clicking and pressing buttons as he controlled events. E-mails flew across the internet and the various web sites gleamed as hits rained down on them. The central control module was a key tool in their work, but equally important were the various pieces of equipment the team used to protect and communicate. The central control module is full of state-of-the-art equipment including credit card-size tele mobiles known as Visi-Tels. These are sophisticated telephone and television devices with ultra-scan techniques used to locate and contact the Surf_Aces who, each have their own Visi-Tel.

The Visi-Tel is mounted on a special material that is coated with a sophisticated sticky substance, a very special film of glue which allows the Visi-Tel to be attached to any part of the Surf_Aces' clothing or skin. The sophisticated glue was invented by DotCombo and the Surf_Aces after finding that if they used Velcro the Visi-Tel could only be attached where they had Velcro on their clothes, it would have been unrealistic to have a completely Velcro based uniform. The glue is known as FLUG, or Finely Laminated Universal Glue to give it its full title. FLUG resists all materials or substances other than that worn or used by DotCombo and the Surf_Aces. FLUG has been programmed to stick to any part of the Surf_Aces, even their skin, hair and equipment. Although if it won't budge DotCombo has the secret antidote! FLUG is waterproof, non absorbent, it has no smell, no taste and is invisible except under a laser-induced beam where it will glow a vibrant flame red.

The formula for FLUG is a closely guarded secret and is only known to DotCombo and the Surf_Aces. There are those who would pay handsomely to have the recipe for FLUG, there are those who would do their utmost to try to steal the formula, like Ram Router!

Ah FLUG, thought DotCombo, *what an invention, one of the best we've ever created.*

'Scanner I need a soft drink, any orange juice in the web fridge?' asked DotCombo.

'Coming right up,' said Scanner whirring around the central control module.

'Scanner, when did we ask the Surf_Aces to be here for the briefing meeting?'

'At 10 a.m. UK web time,' replied Scanner.

'Are you ready, everything prepared?' said DotCombo.

'Yes,' said Scanner. 'Just need to programme the Multiwall and I'm ready.'

'Click!' called DotCombo.

Click turned around flicking switches and pushing buttons, he rose from his chair and surfed over to where DotCombo sat. Click couldn't move in a straight line as he practised his surfing skills at every opportunity, he weaved from side to side around the central control module and the various pieces of equipment. It was from this very distinctive weaving

motion that his code name was developed: Shortcut –
he always took the shortest route!

He wanted to make sure that when the day came
and he would go out on field trials with the Surf_Aces
his surfing abilities would not be in doubt, so he
practised and practised. The only time Click wasn't on
his surfboard was when he was sitting down operating
the central control module, even the surfboard was
hovering ready at his side. He could move in one leap
from his chair on to the surfboard in a flash! Most of
all he liked being called Click, he knew the Surf_Aces
used this as a term of endearment. One day he would
be a proper Surf_Ace.

'DotCombo, I've set up all the controls and once
Scanner has the Multiwall ready I'll get the running
order programmed,' said Click.

'Today you're working the controls, Click,' said
DotCombo.

'Great!' said Click, he liked to work the central
control module.

'Fine, excellent. Good work everyone, let me know,
Scanner, when the Surf_Aces arrive.'

DotCombo settled back into her chair, she relaxed
sipping on the orange drink which Scanner delivered.
The drink was a Tooltip invention. It tasted nothing
like oranges and DotCombo reminded herself to
mention this to Tooltip when the Surf_Aces arrived
for the briefing session. She wasn't sure what it tasted
like, mangoes maybe, or peppermint, but definitely not
oranges!

'It has a kind of smell I can't place either,' she said. 'Scanner what is this orange stuff supposed to be?' she asked.

'Don't know DotCombo, never touch the stuff!' replied Scanner. 'Not my cup of tea, in fact I'd rather have a cup of tea!' chortled Scanner knowing he didn't and couldn't drink anything as he's a robot.

'I don't touch it either,' said Click, 'it makes me walk straight!'

As DotCombo awaited the arrival of the Surf_Aces her mind wandered again. *I like the Visi-Tel, it's so practical and with the FLUG it's much more flexible*, she thought. *I like the way the Visi-Tel can be removed, peeled off easily and quickly which is extremely useful if the Surf_Aces need to remove the Visi-Tel in an emergency or for re-programming, re-charging and replacement.*

The credit card-sized Visi-Tel is also capable of performing a full range of functions from digital picture send/receive, video conferencing, information downloading, web surfing and, most importantly, a sophisticated radar location signal which is very important if the Surf_Ace is in danger. The Visi-Tel can also send and receive e-mail which the Surf_Aces can either view on the Visi-Tel itself, or they can use special spectacles they carry which have an inbuilt digital screen on each lens. This is to allow them to see and send/receive e-mails when they are surfing at high speeds.

Yes, a real multi-purpose device, she thought. *Just as well, we need it. I wonder if Tooltip could hook it up to all the web cameras, must ask him, but only after he explains this juice!*

DotCombo turned her thoughts towards the internet and that menace, her old colleague and now number one enemy, Ram Router.

Ram Router hates the web and everything associated with it.

Ram was in charge of the internet when it was in its infancy in those far off days in the twentieth century when the internet was a United States military communications vehicle/database and e-mail was for designated PC users only. Ram soon discovered the power that access to the internet's knowledge and information would have for those who were in direct control. He was also clever enough to see the enormous possibilities, such as world domination and the opportunity to make large sums of money by stealing data and selling to the highest bidder – of which there were many! Ram wanted control of all the major companies, threatening them with extinction, loss of revenue, stealing their secrets and selling them to competitors. Ram would threaten eventual mass destruction unless they paid large sums of money to him. What a wonderful idea this was and great fun too!

Although he had a high intelligence rating, for some reason he allowed himself to be drawn into a ludicrous scheme. In a none too clever move in 1999 he was caught trying to sell classified information to a group of mad scientists who wanted to take over the internet. Their plan was to use the internet system to release newly programmed, unique contaminated material that would send a doomsday virus into all PC systems as part of their world domination plans.

Once all the PCs were rendered useless the Mad group would have control of all PC manufacture and sales world wide, all software programmes and also the associated revenue – trillions and trillions and trillions of pounds worth! By comparison Bill Gates would be a pauper! But the big catch for all users would be the creation of a new internet only accessible by the Mad group's PCs and software. Watch out Bill Gates and goodbye!

The scheme was exposed when DotCombo inadvertently overheard Ram in a web nightclub boasting about plans and the position of total authority he would enjoy as central control commander of the new internet. DotCombo had a difficult decision to make, sacrificing her relationship with Ram for the protection of the internet.

She reported Ram after firstly telling him of her intentions.

Ram tried to talk her out of it but DotCombo resisted and it broke her heart to see Ram tried as a common criminal. This was one of the most difficult decisions she ever had to make, but she had to. The security of the internet is what she's paid to enforce, her affections for Ram were secondary, and she had to be loyal to her employers too. Ram was now trapped and after a full confession he was taken before the Global Internet Zonal Management Alliance, GIZMA, found guilty and sentenced to live on the periphery of the web for all time.

DotCombo laughed at this point, thinking, *how could he have hoped to get away with it? What a stupid scheme?* DotCombo hesitated. *But if Ram hadn't been so stupid and exposed his plans, albeit by mistake, I wouldn't be sitting in my present position having total authority and be the central control commander.*

'Thanks for being stupid, Ram,' said DotCombo with a glint in her eye.

Ram had tried to place the blame for the failed mad scientist plan on his assistant, Cache Downloader, telling GIZMA at his trial that it was Cache and not him.

'I had nothing to do with it at all, it was Cache who was really to blame,' he pleaded in his defence. 'I was just boasting to impress DotCombo, I'm innocent!'

Although he had no part in the escapade Cache couldn't avoid being implicated because of his long association with Ram and his work on the internet. Ram and Cache had been friends for a long time and had worked closely together setting up the various internet processes and programmes. Many of the innovations and inventions now in every day use on the net were the products of Ram Router and Cache Downloader collaborations. Cache was also the force behind the concept of the Surf_Ace, and in fact was seen as the brains behind the present group of Surf_Aces who had inherited many of his techniques and capabilities. Cache was considered by many to be the first Surf_Ace, a title he did little to dispute and much to promote!

Cache Downloader is a brilliant programmer, but he is first and foremost an adventurer. So it was easy to understand why GIZMA felt he had to have some involvement in Ram Router and the mad scientists' plans.

Although he was innocent Cache was banished by GIZMA, not to the periphery of the web like Ram, but to wander the internet as an outcast. In time Cache Downloader would develop the role of a web mercenary, web treasure seeker, a web hunter, a web pirate who would work for anyone who paid him, he worked for the highest bidder with loyalty to no one. Cache broke off his friendship with Ram and they were never to be associates again. In fact Cache vowed to get even and damage Ram as much as he could and as often as he could in the web years ahead.

Good old Cache, what a guy! thought DotCombo. *I wonder what he's up to these days.*

After the debacle with Ram, DotCombo had developed a high regard for Cache although she knew she could never have strong feelings for him. The situation with Ram meant that never again would she allow her personal feelings to get in the way of her work.

Cache Downloader is attracted to DotCombo but she knows that she'll never let Cache develop this into anything other than friendship, although she does admire his style and likes his infectious smile, quick wit and adventurous ways. Cache was always keen for his attraction towards DotCombo to grow and he would try very hard to impress her whenever he could, although being a wanderer he found it difficult to keep in touch.

Cache really admired the Surf_Aces and would help them whenever he could. Cache particularly liked Refresh whom he felt was the most intelligent of all the Surf_Aces. He saw Refresh as a younger version of himself, he liked Refresh for his style and leadership qualities and their personalities dovetailed perfectly. One day their paths would cross and the truth would be revealed.

Ah Cache, thought DotCombo. *If only…*

Global Internet Zonal Management Alliance, GIZMA is an organisation set up and financed through subscription by World Wide Web users and companies to protect their intellectual property. DotCombo and the Surf_Aces are employed by GIZMA.

Ram was furious at his punishment by GIZMA, even more so when he heard that his former girlfriend, DotCombo, was to be appointed as his replacement, but with even more power and responsibility than empowered to him by GIZMA. Ram also discovered that his most hated enemies, the Surf_Aces, were to be enlisted to assist DotCombo at her specific request. Ram's hatred grew with time and he hated everyone apart from his trusted horde of Bugs who Ram created and produces in the millions in his domain on the periphery of the web. Ram has sworn since his punishment by GIZMA that he would do everything he could to render the internet useless and take it back under his control.

Ram was a popular member of the protection team and he was noted for his original styles. A commanding figure, Ram Router is tall, his dark hair is swept backwards, he's very athletic and wears multicoloured clothes whose colours seem to cascade across his chest. How he does this, no one knows!

He has an evil stare that he uses to great effect on everyone who dares to cross his path. He commands and institutes his evil schemes from his domain, which is only accessible through a giant head that is the very image of Ram himself. It has a large open mouth which is the only way in or out. Ram designed the head entrance and feels it adds glamour and evil to the periphery of the web, it's meant to be frightening and it is!

To help him in his quest for power and control, Ram created an unruly band of Bugs whom he uses to terrorise the whole internet industry. There are zillions and zillions of Bugs and an unlimited production programme maintains their numbers at a level impossible to count. The Bugs obey Ram's every command as he tries to disrupt and destroy incoming/outgoing e-mails, current and new web sites, information stored on the Disks, the Superhighway and hits being made on the web sites.

The Bugs are small and round, sort of onion shaped, with little thin legs, short thin arms and fingers, staring eyes, no nose or ears and a large mouth.

They have long, flexible, wobbly antennae which rises from the top of their head. On top of the antennae a ball is attached, like a small dot it contains their communication capability, a digital radio and a TV screen. This allows them to talk to and see each other and allows Ram to see and hear them via his control desk communicator system. When they want to use the ball they run their hand up the antennae and pull it down to head height in a loop, when they are finished talking or receiving/sending a message they let it go and it snaps back into position like a whip cracking as it wobbles back and forth.

Watching this happen as millions of Bugs speak to each other is an incredible sight and very noisy! Sometimes as they finish communicating and let their antennae go it gets in a fankle and many of the Bugs are tied in knots to each other for long periods!

The Bugs are multicoloured, but each Bug is individually coloured. Not one Bug has the same shade or texture of each colour, some are mixtures of several colours. The ball on top of their antennae is the same colour as their body.

They are able to absorb feelings, movement, sounds, tastes and smells through a little sensor located in their left leg which they lift and shake sideways from time to time to gather information. The left leg sensor helps them to 'hear' signals, sounds and messages coming into their antennae and from situations around them.

As they walk or run and as an introduction to every

statement they make a sound similar to the word 'weeble'. Weeble, weeble, weeble sounds coming from zillions of Bugs is a real big noise!

If Ram could completely destroy the internet he would be extremely pleased. His hatred of the internet originates from his punishment, losing DotCombo and a developing manic desire to control all aspects of the internet and rule the world through misinformation, propaganda, destruction, chaos and, worst of all, fear. He wants his original role of internet protector back but DotCombo now has it, this has made him fanatical about seeking and getting revenge.

Ram and DotCombo were very close, marriage was mentioned on several occasions. After it was discovered that Ram was in fact a criminal and DotCombo had to alert GIZMA to his involvement, it was clear she must have nothing more to do with him.

Ram, Ram, Ram, how could you be so stupid, thought DotCombo, sipping her orange juice or whatever this Tooltip invention was!

Ram Router and the Bugs consider their attacks on the internet as a game, their objective is to create and cause as much disruption and chaos as possible.

They use all means at their disposal and boy do they have an arsenal! They can attack the content of the Disks knowing that the Information Superhighway isn't 100% protected neither are the Disks connected to it. The only level of protection is that which DotCombo and the Surf_Aces provide, and Ram knows this takes a lot of time and effort. DotCombo and the Surf_Aces need to be on their toes, but they can't be everywhere.

The Bugs can, apart from being themselves, become anything, any character, animal, beast, contraption implement they desire and use this ability to good effect. The Bugs can and will introduce into their various attacks any scene or circumstance from an Information Disk, any adventure, space action, wars, cowboys, trains, bombs, gun battles, hordes of wild animals, volcanoes, sharks or action situations and they can even unleash beasts they've designed in their own software programmes.

Ram Router and the Bugs have been known to gatecrash TV programmes shown via the internet and it's not the first time that a news bulletin, quiz or children's show have been badly affected by their evil activities.

They will not hesitate to blast their way into major corporate web sites causing mayhem until the Surf_Aces arrive to clear them out and re-establish order and take control. The Bugs know that the Surf_Aces have their DBMs, which if you're a Bug isn't good news, but ever keen to take on the Surf_Aces they are happy to run the risk of being eliminated. After all, there are zillions more in reserve!

What a bunch thought DotCombo. *Ram Router, former boyfriend and colleague and his Bugs, all sworn enemies of the internet.*

Just as well I've got Click, Scanner and the Surf_Aces or Ram Router and his Bugs would be totally unstoppable. The

Surf_Aces aren't afraid of Ram and the Bugs but they have to be at their best to outwit everything that they have to deal with. She swivelled in her chair and took another sip of orange.

What he will try next and where it will happen are just some of the questions Ram and the Bugs pose everyday… I wonder? She drifted dreamily, the chair moved from side to side as she slowly sipped the orange.

It's been a quiet few web weeks, not much activity, but knowing Ram he'll be up to something, she mused. *Just as well the Surf_Aces are trained for serious danger. When they're surfing around, their speed, ability to move very fast and their accuracy with their DBMs is a huge huge bonus. The Surf_Aces can eliminate the Bugs with their DBMs, but unfortunately there are zillions of Bugs and sometimes when they attack in hordes… WOW!* she thought.

Apart from their various disguises the little rascals will even try to run into a Surf_Ace in an attempt to push them off their magnetic surfboards or foot discs. A Surf_Ace without any means of magnetic surf movement is a sitting target. Surf_Aces can walk and run, they can move like you and I, but without their speed and movement the Bugs have a good opportunity to catch them. And as for that Gloob stuff, what an awful invention, thought DotCombo.

Gloob is the Bugs' big weapon, a wet sticky substance that they fire by bending over, squeezing their hips and firing it from the tip of their antennae. Once a Bug has fired their Gloob they shrivel like a balloon losing all its air and they are flat and useless for almost 7.3 web minutes before they bounce back into shape as more

Gloob is produced inside their little bodies.

If a Surf_Ace is hit with Gloob it affects their speed and ability to move fast and they are in real danger. A Gloobed Surf_Ace is vulnerable. The Surf_Aces are at risk when their speed drops as the Bugs can move in for the kill, so they have to hide and move until they can get help. A Surf_Ace who is Gloobed must try to get back to the central control module before the Gloob sets and hardens completely, only then can DotCombo remove the Gloob, re-charge the Visi-Tel and repair any damages so that the Surf_Ace is ready to do battle once again.

Ram Router and the Bugs would like to capture a Surf_Ace to find out how their magnetic surfboards and foot discs operate, how their DBMs work and figure out what this FLUG stuff is. But more importantly to hold a Surf_Ace is a big prize and a possible opportunity for ransom. If Ram and his Bugs could capture all the Surf_Aces then DotCombo is exposed and the internet is a target for takeover and extortion will run riot. DotCombo would be a real prize capture too and with the Surf_Aces eliminated who could stop Ram from getting direct access to her central control module?

The Bugs will also attack e-mails, web sites, information files and anything that moves on the internet with Gloob. When this happens the data is stopped from any movement and cannot reach its destination address or location in the database. Gloob blocks everything and only when a Surf_Ace can reach the stricken data, remove the Gloob and set it on track to its destination address is the problem solved.

'I wish the Surf_Aces could remove Gloob themselves but the digital current in their DBMs is too deadly, maybe there could be a solution using FLUG,' she mused out loud. 'Must implement this idea, give it a try and see what happens. I must remember to mention it to Tooltip along with the orange juice. Oh, and the Visi-Tel internet camera!

'If every Surf_Ace, every incoming and outgoing e-mail, data file, Disks or whatever is covered in FLUG, the Gloob might not be able to stick, or it may be easier to remove without using the DBMs.'

'Good idea, DotCombo!' said Scanner, listening. 'That was the idea Tooltip suggested a couple of web weeks ago, wasn't it?'

'Yes, you're right Scanner,' said DotCombo. 'Tooltip likes this idea and he says he's some samples to test, I bet he can have it ready soon.' Then DotCombo blushed, a rare occurrence. She had been speaking out loud and hadn't realised. 'You shouldn't be listening Scanner, don't be nosy!'

'It's my job to listen, I'm a Scanner!'

'Well don't scan me Scanner!' said DotCombo laughing.

Well there it is, she thought. *Not a dull moment, the place is full of surprises and danger, no day or adventure will ever be the same with Ram Router and the Bugs on the loose in the internet.*

DotCombo sat upright in her chair and placed her now empty beaker on the module in front of her as she spoke.

'Ram is up to something and we must be ready, the Surf_Aces must be on guard at all times, it is an ongoing battle, a battle we must and will win! If Ram Router and the Bugs succeed, the internet as we know it is doomed and so are we!' she said, followed by a bellow of, 'Scanner, don't listen!'

'I'm not listening,' said Scanner. 'Didn't hear a word. But I agree with you that Ram is up to something, wait until you hear my briefing.'

'Scanner… stop it this web minute, it's at times like this when I could do with an input from Cache Downloader,' said DotCombo. 'He'd know what Ram was up to and it might not be too late for him to have an influence on the future safety and security of the internet,' said DotCombo.

Click, Click. 'There, I double clicked,' said Click. 'I know how you feel, DotCombo, but you can't dwell on the past, you've got the Surf_Aces now and they're more than capable of protecting the internet and anything old Ram Router and his bunch of mindless Bugs have to offer,' said Click reassuringly.

'I know you're right Click, but I can't help thinking that Cache was punished too severely. There's still a job for him here if he ever returns,' said DotCombo.

'But he'd have to behave himself and do as he's told!' snapped Scanner. 'Eh DotCombo?'

'Got it in one Scanner, but it would be nice to see him again.'

'Well, you never know,' said Scanner.

'Yes, you never know,' said Click.

'Thanks for that vote of assurance fellas, we'll see indeed.'

'Right, where are the Surf_Aces? Briefing session starts in two web minutes.'

'They're entering the module screening zone,' said Click.

'I have them on my screens,' said DotCombo. 'I want to start as soon as the Surf_Aces arrive in the central control module. Scanner, get me more of that awful orange juice. All this thinking and dreaming has given me a thirst!' said DotCombo. 'Click, switch on the central control module. Scanner get ready to start the briefing. Multiwall to ON!' she commanded.

Lights flashed as the central control module burst into life, DotCombo had switched it to suspend as she relaxed and now it was time to fire up the system.

'I want a full briefing, Scanner. Give me the latest intelligence from the Ram Router domain, I want to know every movement, every scheme, every breath, every snort, every weeble,' she said. 'I want to know what Ram Router and the Bugs had for breakfast, dinner and supper, I want to know what they didn't have too!' she smiled.

'Click, have the Surf_Aces make their way from the entry zone and into the magnetic security field for screening.'

'Click, Click,' said Click. 'DotCombo, Media has now left the screening area and is about to appear.'

Click had just finished the sentence when Media

appeared, surfing briskly towards DotCombo and the central control module.

'Media, good to see you!' said DotCombo.

'The others should be here right now, get ready – it's show time!' said Media.

Sure enough – in they came – surfing, swivelling, gliding, from side to side, up and over, back flips and shimmies. Refresh, Icon and Tooltip always liked to make a spectacular entrance. 'Nice moves, like the swivel Icon. It's time to go to work, Surf_Aces,' said DotCombo, 'show's over!'

'Hey DotCombo, how's your web day been?' enquired Refresh.

'Just great,' replied DotCombo, forgetting purposely to mention her look back in time.

'DotCombo, have you tried my new orange juice?' said Tooltip. 'It's my latest invention and one of my best by far.'

'Tooltip – I wouldn't know what it was, but take it from me, it's good but not as orange juice!' she laughed and so did Tooltip.

'DotCombo, I've an extra two special passes for the web garage rave next web week,' said Icon. 'I'm taking Kydo, do you want to come, bring a friend?'

'Are the other Surf_Aces going?' asked DotCombo.

'Yes,' they all shouted.

'I'm going too!' said Scanner.

'And me, click, click,' said Click.

'Sure, count me in,' said DotCombo.

'One pass or two?' asked Icon.

'One!' barked DotCombo. 'What would I need with two?'

'We could contact Cache,' said Media, 'I'm sure he'd come since it was you and it was *free*!'

'Leave Cache where he is, wherever he is,' said DotCombo. She sighed, if only! 'Scanner, Click, meeting starts now, Surf_Aces positions please,' said DotCombo. Quickly shrugging off her disappointment at not having an immediate partner for the web garage rave. *Maybe I could send Scanner out to search for Cache and get a message to him*, she thought. *Then again maybe not.*

The Surf_Aces took up their positions around the briefing table.

DotCombo positioned herself at the head, just in front of the central control module where Click sat flicking switches.

'Scanner let's make a start,' said DotCombo.

RAM PREPARES TO STRIKE!

Each day DotCombo summons her Surf_Aces to a meeting. Click, under DotCombo's instructions, will have made a formal request for the Surf_Aces to be present. DotCombo enjoys these briefings and uses them to keep up to date not only with events, but also each Surf_Ace.

Although they have a dangerous job the Surf_Aces, their thirst for living and fun, DotCombo finds irresistible. She had chosen this group well. Their enthusiasms rub off on everyone they come into contact with and their company extremely enjoyable. They could also be serious and ruthless, particularly when it came to protecting the web. They believed that if you work hard you needed to play hard too and in this they saw making fun and having a good time as a perfect balance.

At the meeting Scanner will cover recent events and will provide an overview of current problems, situations and intelligence he has picked up as he searches the web. Scanner will inform the group of anticipated activity by Ram Router and his Bugs. He will try to provide them with as much information as possible in detailed briefing formats to allow DotCombo and the Surf_Aces to react positively and quickly to any threat.

Scanner will use a series of several thousand projector screens mounted on a high banking, which formed part of the main wall of DotCombo's central control module. It was impressive when in use and Scanner enjoyed these sessions because he could display his search results in glorious digital colour and stereo surround sound.

Scanner calls it his Multiwall, he is proud of this instrument which he operates by a laser beam he shoots from his scanning head. He uses the laser to point and highlight his information, changing the images as he scrolls through his pitch.

DotCombo will issue instructions to the Surf_Aces based on the information presented by Scanner and the ensuing discussion. She will ask for advice and guidance. DotCombo respects her Surf_Aces and their views and opinions are very important to her. Normally she will give them instructions to patrol a specific area or location if it's believed that an attack is imminent.

Sometimes they will have to react instantly to a situation developing during their briefing session. The Surf_Aces liked unplanned activity as it was always different and exciting.

If no disruption is anticipated or low risk information is all that's available, DotCombo will allow the Surf_Aces to patrol a site, zone or area which she believes will occupy and interest them whilst they await further instructions. This is always good news for the Surf_Aces as usually it allows them a lot of time to explore new places, new lands, new information and, most of all, lots of play time! Surf_Aces like to play and the web is a giant playground with so much to do and see.

However, Ram Router and his Bugs are always active and up to something. DotCombo and Scanner have heard that they plan an attack on the Animal Kingdom Disk. What they plan to do is unknown but you can be sure it will be serious and could put the animals and/or their environment in danger.

It is also not known which breed of animal, country or even geography they will attack. Current intelligence and a recent attack by Ram and his Bugs on e-mails and web sites where animal welfare and known charities are featured could be a possible clue to their next move.

Refresh and Tooltip were involved in this attack. Every e-mail and web site hit by litres of Gloob. E-mails were stuck in transit, web sites were unreadable, the internet itself almost ground to a halt. Worst of all, anyone logging on to any of these sites while the attack was in progress had the Gloob virus downloaded into their PC system. What a mess! DotCombo had to send out a special programme fix to all users to allow their systems to re-boot.

Tooltip was Gloobed during the attack. A large group of Bugs cornered him in the AdventureLand Disk where the Bugs had gone to hide. He had to be rescued by Media just as Ram moved into capture him. Tooltip had a very lucky escape. The AdventureLand Disk is an exciting place, but it has its dangers. The

Bugs were on the run and were being followed closely by Tooltip. He was travelling at around six quantum calamities and catching up on them fast. Suddenly they disappeared into the Rocky Mountains, a place where they intended to hide until it was safe.

The Rocky Mountains are a long mountain range located on the West Coast of the United States. They run almost the complete length of the country north to south. The mountains are vast and very difficult to navigate.

The Rockies, as they are known, are home to a host of animals, geographical wonders and plant life not found in any other part of the world.

In the nineteenth century as expeditions of settlers tried to find a route from the east to west they had to endure much hardship, attacks by wild animals, long hot spells and below zero temperatures.

None of this interested Tooltip at the moment as he skimmed the surface of the mountains looking for the Bugs. Strangely, he could feel himself being watched. Maybe he was wrong, but it bothered him and as he looked over his shoulder his eye nearly popped! He was right, he was being watched! Cyber Crows, thousands of them, were coming straight for him.

A Bug invention, the Cyber Crow is a dangerous customer as they swoop, peck and jab at you with their metal beaks. Tooltip weaved in and out of the crevices between each mountain, but no matter how hard he tried he couldn't shake them off. He could feel them, he could see their piercing eyes, and he could smell their digital breath. No matter how hard he tried he could not get away from them. They swarmed all around him. Their computer generated beaks pecked and jabbed at him. He fired his DBM but each shot missed, how could they move about with such ease?

What Tooltip didn't know and couldn't yet see was the new control panel designed by Ram Router. The Bugs were operating the Cyber Crows from a ledge high up in the mountains, just where the ice and snow begins to form. If Tooltip could get to the Bugs he had a chance to attack them.

He dived at speed hoping the crows would follow, they did.

Then suddenly he swerved at an angle and launched himself upwards. 'Eight quantum calamities,' he shouted. 'Catch me now!'

The speed Tooltip generated and his surfing movements were too fast for the Bugs and their control panel. The Bugs twiddled and bashed their little control panels to no effect. Tooltip's surfing speed and his swerving movements and twists were too fast for them to duplicate. The Cyber Crows were in a real fankle and started to bang into each other. As they lost height and direction, they fell crashing into the ravine below with an almighty smash followed by a massive electrical storm of sparks flying upwards and outwards at all angles.

It was an incredible sight, like the fireworks display Tooltip had seen recently in the Y2K Millennium Celebrations Disk.

Tooltip fights the Cyber Crows

Worse was to follow though, the upward draft projected Tooltip too close to the Bugs and as he tried to deflect himself away he was Gloobed!

Stuck fast to a ledge with the Bugs on the way down, Tooltip just managed to send out a location signal and a danger tone via his Visi-Tel.

Media was the first to pick up the danger tones. She was enjoying herself in the Health and Beauty Disk having a warm jacuzzi.

She sourced Tooltip's signal as coming from the AdventureLand Disk and immediately, well almost immediately – the jacuzzi was too good to stop, she was on her way. Media knew she had to hurry, a danger tone is a priority one emergency.

Tooltip was now stuck fast, in deep trouble and about to be captured by Ram who had arrived on hearing the good news about a Surf_Ace in danger and properly Gloobed.

Media surfed from the Health and Beauty Disk, up the Information Superhighway and on to the internet, carefully surfing in and out of e-mails Gloobed to the spot. She decided it would be quicker to head for the AdventureLand Disk by way of the New World of Transport Disk, which had only recently been added to the web.

'Wow! There goes a 1986 electric train, and look, a coach and horses!' she cried. *I bet the electric train was more comfortable*, she thought as she surfed past. She waved at the passengers on the train who were surprised but pleased to wave back. What must they be thinking as they saw her surfing past in mid-air at high speed? Media was just visible as she shot past. 'Hey, what's that?' she exclaimed. 'It must be a rickshaw, that weird three-wheeled contraption used in China and some Asian countries. It's pulled by a man, with seating for two passengers,' she whispered to herself. *How did they ever get anywhere in that*? she thought, accelerating to eight quantum calamities. Little did she know that rickshaw transport was still in existence! Transport had really evolved. Firstly from hand and foot to steam, then petrol and electricity and now, in the twenty-first century magnetic digital laser surfing.

Out of the Transport Disk, she quickly found the AdventureLand Disk and skimmed the surface whilst looking for Tooltip. She knew the Rocky Mountains were somewhere, but in which direction? The Visi-Tel signal was a little weak now but just strong enough to allow her to get a directional sound byte.

'Beautiful countryside this!' she called, her voice echoed, bouncing off mountain after mountain. 'Surf_Aces surf the best!' she called, enjoying the echo and the sound of her own voice. 'Media loves Refresh!' she shouted over and over at the top of her voice, as the echoes overlapped on top of one another causing a huge wall of noise.

Suddenly, there was Tooltip stuck to a ledge. He did look funny, but with the Bugs and now Ram Router hot on his trail she couldn't waste any time. Gloob was a difficult substance to deal with.

It wasn't glue. It wasn't a liquid. It was like a cross

between a very thick mud and raspberry jam, but it was blue! She didn't want to use her DBM as this would harm Tooltip.

If she could get a hold of him she could perhaps manoeuvre him off the ledge and, if this worked, he might stick to her. They could make their escape bonded together.

The Bugs had other ideas. They bombarded Media with Gloob.

She did her best to surf in and out of the ledges that gave her some cover as she tried to pluck Tooltip off the ledge he was stuck to.

Gloob flew about everywhere in an uncontrolled frenzy, sticking to trees, birds, in fact – everything in sight.

Little deflated Bugs lay busily making new Gloob.

It was an odd sight when a Bug fired their Gloob and then fell to the ground, flattened and squirming about trying to make more Gloob as fast as possible inside the normal 7.3 web minutes. As they finished they would then bounce up and start shaking their left leg as they tried to reset their sensors and hurry back into battle ready to Gloob again!

'Weeble, weeble, weeble!' the Bugs cried as they grew excited and jumped up and down, shaking their left legs in excitement as they soaked up the moment.
Media had a look at their position and decided to see if she could hit the ledge they stood on with her DBM. If she could strike the bottom corner it would shatter, and the Bugs would fall hundreds of feet to the canyon

below. First blast, missed. Next blast, she hit a Bug which leapt up in the air, somersaulted and disappeared over the edge screaming, 'Weeble, weeble, weeble…'

Media laughed, this sound always struck her as being extremely funny.

'Weeble, weeble, weeble, some more you Bug menaces!' she shouted and fired another blast from her DBM.

Blast! This time the ledge crumpled into pieces, the Bugs tried to leap to another ledge but the force of the blast carried them outwards, and to Media's relief, downwards. She blasted at the general area again and again just to make sure there were no footholds for the Bugs to jump back on to. Weeble, weeble, weeble, weeble, weeble sounds filled the air as a horde of Bugs fell over the edge and down into the ravine below.

Ram shouted, 'You've had it Media, you'll pay for this!'

Ram couldn't get near Tooltip or Media as the ledge she had blasted was the only one near to both of them and too far for Ram to jump from his position.

Media grabbed Tooltip and as he was peeled off the ledge he promptly stuck to her.

'It worked,' she said pleased with herself.

Joined almost at the hip they headed at great speed up and over the mountains, out of the information tracks and at last out of the AdventureLand Disk. This was a lucky escape, the Bugs and Ram were much too close for comfort and the Surf_Aces knew that only the quick intervention of Media had saved Tooltip from certain capture, or even destruction. It took DotCombo several hours to clean the Gloob off Tooltip and prepare him for further battles.

'So beware,' said DotCombo as she closed the briefing session and sent the Surf_Aces out on patrol.

It was to be a good day. DotCombo wanted the Surf_Aces to patrol the Toytown and Playland Disk area and assorted children's information zones on the web for a couple of hours and then they were to head for the Animal Kingdom Disk in case Ram Router and the Bugs attacked.

'I'll have Scanner complete another search of the web,' said DotCombo, 'and if I need you, Click will send a message to the Visi-Tels. Oh, and Surf_Aces? Please behave yourselves in the children's zones.'

'Yes you can be sure we will!' cried the Surf_Aces. 'You can be sure we will!'

The Surf_Aces swerved and weaved, gliding over and under each other as they surfed off onto the Superhighway and in the direction of the children's zones. Refresh was the first to arrive.

'I fancy trying the new multi dipper,' he shouted to the others as they arrived.

The multi dipper was a giant ride constructed entirely of plastic which had an amazing fifty double upturns, fourteen underwater dips and, for good measure, a ten web kilometre long upside-down tunnel of disaster.

This sounded like everything a Surf_Ace could

want for a few hours' play.

'Let's do that later, Refresh,' said Media. 'What about Story Teller Disk?' she continued. 'I like a good story.'

'Great idea,' said Icon, he had a girlfriend in the Story Teller Disk who prepared the stories for publishing on the various book club web sites.

A visit to Story Teller Disk would give him an opportunity to see her.

Her name was Kydo, short for Kaleidoscope. Her parents were new age internet programmers and they thought this was a thoroughly modern name for the twenty-first century. Kydo liked her full name, but preferred the shorter version as her nickname. Icon liked her name too, but most of all he really liked her.

She was very pretty with dark features and was full of fun and extremely boisterous. She liked games, particularly children's games and stories. She requested a preference to work on the Story Teller site and was currently taking a course to become a webmaster. Kydo could tell a really good story and always had new ones to hand from the vast catalogue included in the Story Teller Disk.

She also liked it when the Surf_Aces patrolled this zone because they were fun and exciting.

Kydo's parents had been of mixed origin. Her father was of Japanese/Australian stock and her mother was European with parents who originated from Africa. In Kydo's appearance her mixed lineage showed! Kydo was beautiful, a real cracker. Ask Icon, ask any of the

Surf_Aces. Icon hoped that one day she would become a Surf_Ace. Kydo wasn't aware of this.

'Hey Kydo!' shouted Media. 'We're on patrol here for a few hours, good to see you. What's new?'

'I've got a new "Bobler" book.'

'Yeah!' cried all the Surf_Aces. 'Knockout, we'll do this then try the multi dipper!' they called excitedly to one another.

The Surf_Aces liked 'Bobler'. 'Bobler' was a round, fluffy, humorous little person. A bouncy character, a cross between a koala bear and a hamster. He was always getting into silly situations and he was very popular with all the children so his escapades always had an important message or a lesson for them at the end. He had his own web site too 'www.bobler.supernet.com'.

Ram and the Bugs had threatened to hit Bobler's web site. They didn't like his wholesome charm and popularity with children and, of course, as he was popular with the Surf_Aces too, it was a perfect excuse for Ram and the Bugs to attack. An attack would come on Bobler, but when!

'Can we hear the new story, Kydo?' Tooltip who had surfed up behind her and then whizzed past making her black hair rise up on end.

'Hey Spikey!' called Tooltip.

'I'll Spikey you,' Kydo laughingly responded. 'If you have time, how about this one as it will only take five minutes,' said Kydo.

'Okay, let's hear it,' said Refresh.

'It's called "Bobler and The New Lawn",' said Kydo.

'Surf down into the zone and we'll make a start,' she continued.

'Ready?' Kydo asked.

'Let's go Bobler!' shouted the Surf_Aces.

'Bobler and The New Lawn,' said Kydo. Bobler thought that he would take a walk into the park today.

The air was fresh and the sky was clear, a beautiful blue with little cirrus clouds scattered around. *A lovely day for a walk* he thought. A little song ran though his mind.

'Where's the sun, I see it shine, the sun is bright, please be mine.'

'There's a lot of warmth and a jolly good time for everyone when the sun shines.'

He then started to whistle, no particular tune, just a series of noises and soon Bobler was in the park.

It was a large park full of grass, trees and lots of people.

Bobler, still whistling, wandered over in the direction of a small pond.

Look at those kids paddling in the pond, they'll scare the fish and ducks, he thought.

I'll call to them to stop.

'Hey, you're scaring the fish and ducks!' he shouted.

'What fish and ducks?' a small boy replied.

'The fish and ducks in the pond,' exclaimed Bobler.

'If you come out now they'll come back and we can

see them swimming.'

'We're not coming out,' they all shouted, 'the water's great!'

'Here comes the park keeper,' said Bobler. 'He'll chase you.'

'Quick, let's go. He's right!' they called to one another.

As the park keeper came closer all the kids ran off. As Bobler turned to say hello to him he had forgotten how close he was to the edge of the pond and he slipped straight in with a great splash.

The park keeper was furious and ran towards him.

Bobler spluttered, 'I was trying to get the kids to come out when I fell in myself.'

'Oh really,' said the park keeper.

'Yes honest,' said Bobler, standing wet through and now in a large and growing puddle as he dripped.

'You're soaking,' said the park keeper. 'Come on, let's go and dry you off.'

Thankfully the park keeper believed Bobler and they chatted as they walked to his cabin. The park keeper walked into his cabin to get a towel and Bobler waited outside. Watching the passers-by, he wandered a few metres to the side of the cabin.

Bobler was engrossed in the scene so much he didn't realise; he was walking onto and across the park keeper's new lawn!

As he returned with a towel the park keeper called, 'Oh my goodness, look where you are now!'

Bobler was on the new lawn, he had grass seed

stuck to his feet and he was sinking into the new soft earth. Being wet through, his clothes weighed him down and Bobler was slowly sinking!

'Help, I'm sinking,' he cried. 'Quick get a rope, get something!' Bobler said panicking.

'Hold on, I'll pull you out,' said the park keeper.

Try as he could the park keeper couldn't budge Bobler. Bobler was too heavy.

'Hey kids, come over here,' shouted the park keeper, 'I need help.'

The kids ran towards the lawn and, linking arms with the park keeper, they pulled Bobler from the muddy squelch.

'Look at my new lawn,' said the park keeper. 'Look what you've done.'

'What about me?' said Bobler. 'I look like a giant hedge!'

'I'll have to start digging and planting again,' the park keeper said sadly.

'You helped me so I'll help you,' said Bobler.

The kids shouted, 'Can we help too?'

'Yes, of course,' said Bobler.

'I owe you a favour,' said Bobler to the park keeper. 'It's a lovely day, the sun is warm, I'll dry soon and it shouldn't take long to dig, rake the ground and then replant more seed.'

Bobler and the kids worked really hard and soon the new lawn was as good as before. Bobler and the kids enjoyed a cool drink of lemonade with the park keeper before they left for home.

Today had been exciting as well as good fun, thought Bobler.

He reflected on having shouted at the kids. There were no fish and ducks in the pond at all, the park keeper told him as they walked back to the cabin. If it hadn't been for the kids how would he have been rescued from the sinking mud? Bobler had learned a lesson today.

He thought, *always know your facts before you speak out and don't be harsh on others when you don't know what you're talking about.*

I've learned a good lesson today, thought Bobler. *I think the kids did too; without them I'd have been still stuck!*

Bobler smiled as he considered his day in the park and the new lawn that he'd almost wrecked by himself, he laughed loudly and walked off whistling his little tune, nothing in particular just a series of whistling noises.

'And that's the story, The End,' said Kydo.

'What a great old fashioned story,' said Media. 'I liked it a lot.'

'What a good message for children everywhere,' said Icon.

'Okay Surf_Aces, back to work,' said Refresh. 'We've a job to do.'

'See you Kydo!' they shouted as they surfed off.

'Kisses and hugs for Icon,' said Icon.

'Next time, Icon,' said Kydo as she headed back into the zone, 'next time, if you're really good.'

The Surf_Aces waved goodbye to Kydo and headed

off out of the Story Teller Disk and back on patrol. They really enjoyed Kydo and her stories.

'Let's go back tomorrow,' said Icon. 'I'd like to see Kydo again.'

'Oh, I love you Kydo,' said Refresh mimicking Icon's voice then raising his speed to four quantum calamities. He shot off ahead, and the others followed, laughing.

GLOOB

Sitting in his fortress located on the periphery of the web Ram Router had other ideas. He and his Bugs were planning a visit to the Animal Kingdom Disk to cause trouble, lots of trouble. Ram's domain, a virtual fortress, was on the outer reaches of the web, literally on the outer edge – oblivion, as Ram was sometimes known to call it.

It was a world so different from anything else. Entry was through a giant head built in the image of Ram, it had a large open mouth and staring eyes. It was a frightening sight as it towered over the horizon; in fact it towered over everything.

All the down level and out-of-date files and records are sent here, it's the web trash can. If a PC user hits the delete button on their keyboard, the trash can is where the unwanted information or data goes. Ram is almost up to his multicoloured neck in rubbish and refuse.

He is surrounded by old hard drives complete with data, circuit boards, keyboards, monitors, software commands, corrupt data files, old game formats, programmes, deleted e-mails, presentation material, discarded animation and old documents. Worst maybe of all, lots and lots of discarded viruses!

The junkyard of the internet is home to Ram and his Bugs.

domain is littered with Gloobed e-mails, Gloobed letters, Gloobed numbers, Gloobed pictures, Gloobed equipment and Gloobed personal computers, in fact, just about everything in the domain has Gloob attached to it somewhere.

Gloob is everywhere, stuck to walls, it's stuck to Bugs who are stuck to each other as they tried to master their firing skills and their early attempts at hitting the target failed miserably. In mock battles and pranks the Bugs would fire Gloob at each other, sometimes with deadly results as Bugs became stuck fast with no means of becoming un-Gloobed!

Despite its outward severe and unwelcoming exterior inside, Ram's domain is bright. It has to be with zillions of multicoloured Bugs all over the place and, of course, Ram himself is an extremely colourful character, even if he is fearsome! It is a world apart, odd, in a strange way and colourful. Yet at times, if Ram was in a foul mood, it could be dark and very unpleasant.

The whole domain is lit by darting laser beams that Ram positioned at various strategic places around his domain. The laser beams are old versions, like the kind used in early 1970s pop shows, concerts and discos. They spread green and blue flashes everywhere, such was their clever positioning and power the whole place seemed alight with vibrant colour. Mix this with Ram's multicoloured clothes, the Bugs themselves and wow, was this place bright!

The Bugs are everywhere, weeble, weeble, weeble,

mayhem is on the loose all over the domain as the Bugs play or fight with each other on trampolines, on tiny electric go-carts, swings, chutes and roundabouts. The noise is deafening and sometimes Ram has to shout loud to make himself heard above the chaos. To make matters worse, the Bugs are always inventing new ideas, deadly weapons or some mind-bending scam from all the trash and rubbish which litters the domain. They don't hesitate to try out the latest ploys on each other and loud explosions can be heard. Cries of 'weeble, weeble, weeble' ring out excitedly, and sometimes painfully all over the place.

That's why Ram and the Bugs are in their element in the domain, all this mayhem, trash and old junk has a purpose, it just needs to be found or invented. Ideas and inventions, new and old, lie all over the domain, some cast off as useless, some half finished and waiting for a spark of genius to bring it to life. The Bugs invent things that are hopeless. Some of their most recent failures are semi-magnetic surfboards that can only move backwards and to the side, not forward. In the trials Bugs were bashing into each other, bouncing off the walls, in fact bouncing off everything mobile or static. When a group of them collided with Ram's console that was the end of the wandering surfboard.

He set fire to the surfboards with a series of blasts from his Snort-gun, a peculiar device he stole from Cache Downloader. It looks like an old space gun, it fires laser beams but it also has a built in zapper device

61

which can fire exploding pellets rapidly and at high speed.

If his aim is good it can be extremely accurate and deadly.

Bugs bounced off each other as the exploding pellets rained down on them. Ram was a good shot. He rarely missed once his aim was fixed.

Each shot, if it hit its target, would explode causing the Bug and the surfboard to catch fire quickly. Ram didn't miss often and the air was filled with 'weeble, weeble, weeble' shrieks as the Bugs were zapped and their surfboards burst into flame.

'This is a better idea than I first thought,' said Ram. 'I thought a new form of transport, not a shooting game,' he laughed loudly.

And so the Bugs surfboard invention went up in smoke!

Undaunted, the Bugs pressed on and the ideas went from bad to worse. Exploding lollipops, exploding smells and weapons that didn't work which they made out of old PC bits and pieces. The Bugs produced a warbling stunner that let off a mind-bending tone meant to drive the victim mad, unfortunately it worked on everybody including Ram. The sounds almost drove him over the edge and he was up and at them with his Snort-gun again! However, for every new idea or invention that didn't work, there were plenty that did. Just wait until you see what they come up with as our story unfolds.

In Ram Router's domain one of the best inventions

ever produced was Gloob. Gloob was developed from an idea of Ram's. Well it wasn't really an idea for Gloob; he stumbled upon the properties of Gloob by mistake. He was actually trying to invent a new super drink by combining raspberry jam and a liquid stuff that resembled mud.

What he eventually produced was a substance that stuck to everything so fast that nothing could remove it, not even soap and water!

Ram saw a great future for Gloob as an attack weapon and had instructed the Bugs to find an innovative method of propelling it forward, i.e. delivering it to its target.

Various attempts failed, like firing it from an electric canon. The voltage was too high and the whole thing backfired, covering hundreds of Bugs in Gloob. A huge mound can still be seen in the domain which is actually the pile of Gloobed Bugs!

Another idea was to put the Gloob into plastic bags, swing them round and round and throw them through the air at the intended victim. Unfortunately this method had its drawbacks. As the Bugs swung the Gloob filled plastic bags above their heads, their antennae would pierce the bag just as they let go, Gloobing them to it and propelling them forward attached to the plastic bag. So the Bug became Gloobed to wherever the bag flew or whatever it struck! Bugs were stuck headfirst to walls, to each other, to just about everything! There were plastic bags Gloobed to the different levels with little Bugs stuck in mid air their legs and arms waving about like crazy! One multicoloured Bug whirled around so fast with the plastic bag whizzing above his head that he flew off into the distance, 'weeble, weeble, weeble,' and promptly Gloobed himself to a flock of Cyber Crows who were passing overhead. He hasn't been seen since! Although word has come back that he and fifty Cyber Crows are Gloobed to the Sydney Harbour Bridge located in the Adventure Stories with Skippy in the Australia Land Disk!

Finally, a bright green Bug stepped forward and said, 'Weeble, weeble, weeble, why don't we drink the Gloob, well it was meant to be a drink anyway, and use our antennae as the firing mechanism? Weeble, weeble, weeble, by squeezing our hips with our hands the Gloob could be pushed out and if we push hard enough we'll get quite a distance.' He continued, 'Weeble, weeble, weeble, not only that, but I'll bet if we used the antennae we could get a better aim too since we would point it at our target. It wouldn't be like our previous ideas when we couldn't direct the Gloob properly,' said the bright green Bug confidently.

'What a great idea,' said Ram. 'How about not only do you drink it, but we develop a way of manufacturing the Gloob inside each Bug. Anyone got any ideas how we set about this?' asked Ram.

'Weeble, weeble, weeble, I do,' said a pink spotted Bug, who had stepped out from the crowd. 'If we convert the Gloob into a tablet form we can then take loads of tablets.'

'Immediately following our Gloob firing, the tablets would instantly make more Gloob,' said the pink Bug with spots. 'Weeble, weeble, weeble, once we Gloob something or,' he laughed, 'someone, we would make more Gloob in about 7.3 web minutes if my calculations are accurate,' continued the pink spotted Bug.

'So what are you saying,' said Ram, 'the Bugs load up on these Gloob tablets before going out on an attack and they could attack all day?

'But once the tablets are finished, then what happens?' Ram asked inquisitively with a firm fixed stare. The stare frightened everybody. Left legs shook in unison, antennas swished back and forth.

'Weeble, weeble, weeble, if the tablets are all finished the Bug will stay floppy, flat and useless. But there's zillions of us Ram, so what if we lose a few Bugs?' said the pink Bug with spots.

'You're a right little pink menace when you get going, with no scruples either,' said Ram. 'I like you, you've got a mean and nasty streak. We need more of your kind in here. Right, that's settled. We make Gloob tablets and each Bug stocks up on them before going out,' said Ram banging on his console with his closed fist.

'Weeble, weeble, weeble' cries were everywhere as the news spread of this super new attack weapon. None of the Bugs considered the implication of running out of Gloob!

Gloob is only a small part of the ideas and inventions

created. Ram and the Bugs have also stumbled upon numerous uses for all the trash in their domain. Old software programmes, games and processes can be re-generated and turned into devious contraptions, devices and viruses which can attack the web sites, the Disks and, of course, DotCombo and her famous Surf_Aces. Rare and defunct game monsters, tools and old programmes are extremely useful. They are ancient and as a result many of today's modern and up to the minute programmes and software packages don't have the ability to deal with them. No one had considered that they would ever be required or used again when they were originally trashed, so the ability to deal with them is almost zero. Nothing is built into the current PCs and Disks to counteract them.

The situation is similar to the problem raised in the final years of the twentieth century regarding the well documented 'Millennium Bug' which required significant financial investment, software upgrades and complex programming to fix. Even with this investment, no one could really be sure all would be fine as the year 2000 arrived. In the end at midnight on the 31 December 1999 everything was okay, or was it? Only time would tell.

Here in the trash was a vast array of somewhat archaic but potentially deadly weapons. A piece of the 'old' PC world which could be used to attack and disrupt the 'new' PC world. In the wrong hands the contents of the trash could be a source of unlimited trouble and disaster. In Ram Router and his Bugs, the right person and the right team of saboteurs was in place not only to seek, find and develop this potential, but also with a manic determination to unleash this on an unsuspecting community, the internet users. There was danger everywhere and anywhere now with the in-bred capabilities of Ram and his Bugs coupled to an ability to put to good use the technology of yesterday to wreak havoc on the internet.

The latest potentially dreadful new invention was now ready.

The Bugs had taken a piece of an old 1986 vintage memory processor game based on hide and seek. They had matched it with a killer PC virus from the late 1990s and produced a monster of epic proportions which they've named the Happy Virus. Once the Happy Virus is downloaded into a recipient's PC it will flood onto all the software. Once inside, the Happy Virus sits waiting until a particular programme, data file or game is requested by the user. As the software activates onto the display screen the Happy Virus activates.

The Bugs have produced roughly two hundred devices containing the Happy Virus, actual figures are hard to establish, the real number could be significantly higher. In the region of forty-five have been released into the web. Eleven made it to their destination addresses.

Basically, it's a very simple virus. It causes the PC programme to jump up and down with laughter, scream with laughter and cry with laughter until it reaches breaking point. At which stage the programme makes a high-pitched laughter tone, explodes and dies through sheer joy and ecstasy.

The PC user's file is gone, dead. The Happy Virus sits hiding in the software and waits for the next programme to be activated and so on, until the PC is useless.

There is no known cure, only intervention before arrival can stop it. As the Bugs send out the Happy Virus through the internet it can be detected. It has an Achilles heel. As it progresses through the internet it giggles and laughs all the time, an extremely annoying function. Spreading itself out in all directions into and across the internet, the noise can be most irritating. Everyone who has heard it has to immediately put their fingers into their ears to block out the awful sound. DotCombo and the Surf_Aces watch and listen for this and can kill the virus with their DBMs, but they can't catch them all and unfortunately some do escape. Scanner has a special duty to make sure an emergency alert is sounded the very moment any Happy Virus movement or noise occurs. The Bugs will launch the Happy Virus at incoming and outgoing e-mails and data files. It's been known for the Happy Virus to score a direct hit on an e-mail, with the result that before the e-mail can reach its destination address it dies of laughter.

The Happy Virus can't yet be deployed directly into a Disk or even onto the Information Superhighway. However, intelligence gathered by Scanner indicates that Ram and the Bugs are about six web months away from having a prototype ready for trial, which means that a usable Happy Virus could be ready in less than twelve months. If they can achieve this then a new and sinister danger will arrive on the internet posing a new threat for DotCombo and the Surf_Aces to deal with.

Ram didn't have thoughts at the moment for the Happy Virus although he knew this was a great and potent weapon, his immediate thoughts and top priorities were aimed at the Animal Kingdom Disk. A very rare tiger featured in the latest Disk that DotCombo had recently released onto the web as an upgrade to the original Disk.

This was to give users an insight into the problems the rare tiger faces in the real world through extinction, hunting and the relentless pursuit of the animal for its priceless skin and teeth. The authors of the new Disk wanted to stimulate interest and hopefully promote greater awareness which would lead to tougher controls by governments and animal rights institutions around the world.

They also hoped to raise more money to finance additional rangers in the national parks across areas where extinction was a real possibility. A web site was in the planning stages where web surfers could get the latest information, contact a direct infoline and purchase CDs, books and order soft toys, replica caricatures and pictures about the tigers using their credit cards.

Ram wanted the tigers as a ransom tool. Ram

wanted the rare tigers very badly. If they were as rare as he was led to believe, then he might be able to draw the Surf_Aces into a series of traps and maybe capture one or all of them. DotCombo would do anything to get back her precious Surf_Aces.

Perhaps he could catch that little sneak Scanner who was always spying on Ram and the Bugs.

'Bugs!' shouted Ram.

'Weeble, weeble, weeble,' sounds came from over the horizon. In the region of eight million Bugs appeared.

'Just as well I didn't shout louder,' said Ram. 'Goodness knows how many of you would have appeared!'

'Listen, there's a rare tiger in the new Animal Kingdom Disk and I want them.'

'Weeble, weeble, weeble, weeble, weeble, weeble,' the Bugs jumped up and down shaking their left legs in anticipation, antennae swishing back and forward and from side to side. Can you picture eight million Bugs doing this, all in unison?

One Bug bent over and sneezed. Gloob flew out of its antennae and the Bug standing immediately in front was Gloobed to the spot!

'Watch what you're doing,' said Ram. 'You just missed me, this stuff is dangerous enough without Gloobing each other or me. Right, the first Bug to Gloob me has had it!' he raged. As if to prove his point Ram walked over to the crowd where a couple of Bugs stood. Without any warning Ram lifted his foot and with lightning movement squashed both Bugs flat. They made a sprafff, splodge, splat sound as they were flattened into a heap. Gloob shot out of their antennae and across the floor.

'Now!' shouted Ram. 'Keep your Gloob for attacks on DotCombo, the internet and those Surf_Aces!' he bellowed. 'The next Bug who splurts that stuff near me is a goner.'

The Bugs went 'weeble, weeble, weeble' altogether and shook their left legs. They'd got the message, but being accident prone it was only a matter of time before Gloob would make its mark on Ram.

The two flattened Bugs suddenly sprung back to life in the regulation 7.3 web minutes. Fortunately they were both well stocked up on Gloob tablets!

Since the Bugs had no natural leader or spokesperson, Ram assumed this role on their behalf and no Bug ever chose to question it.

The usual routine they all recognised was that a Bug would step forward, 'weeble, weeble, weeble,' and ask a question, make a point, make a suggestion or announce some new and fantastic invention and then step back into the crowd. Any Bug could step forward, there was no hierarchy, no standing on ceremony and the Bugs were all equal and each had their own thoughts and views which they were never ever slow to express. It was this informality and unwritten code that held the Bugs in check. They knew that Ram was always up for new ideas, inventions and creations. A Bug who had an idea would never hesitate to step forward and announce it. Sometimes an idea was hatched by a large number of Bugs who would step forward and announce it in unison, this had to be seen and heard!

A red Bug stepped out of the assembled horde. 'Weeble, weeble, weeble Ram, weeble, weeble, weeble,' it said, left leg shaking vigorously. 'How do you plan to capture the tiger?' it asked. The Bug stepped back into the ranks. 'Weeble, weeble, weeble.'

'I want a special Gloob, extra sticky, but it mustn't damage the tiger's fur. We'll slip into the Animal Kingdom Disk when those Surf_Aces are playing or having their team talks with,' and with his teeth clenched Ram spat, 'DotCombo.'

A green Bug with odd multicoloured spots stepped forward. 'Weeble, weeble, weeble, weeble,' shook his left leg and said, 'I did an extra weeble there,' it chuckled. 'Why don't we create a diversion? DotCombo will send the Surf_Aces to see what's happening and during their absence we slip into the Disk, weeble, weeble, weeble,' left leg shake, 'weeble, weeble,' and it stepped back into the crowd.

'Fabulous, extra weeble or not, you can weeble as much as you like if you come up with ideas like that. Any more ideas that we could try?' said Ram.

The sound of 'weeble, weeble, weeble' filled the air. The noise was deafening.

'Quiet, quiet,' shouted Ram.

'Weeble, weeble, weeble,' they continued.

Ram picked up a laser gun he had found at the old

Star Wars game site which had arrived in the trash a few years ago. Pointing it into the crowd of Bugs he shouted, 'Quiet down or I fire!'

Millions of left legs shook in fear and the noise stopped.

'Thanks goodness for that. Now, one at a time.'

A brown Bug said, 'Weeble, weeble, weeble, why don't we lay a trap in the HistoryLand Disk? We could send out misinformation, Scanner will pick it up and report it to DotCombo who'll send the Surf_Aces.

'Let's pretend that we're going to the Disk to release a herd of Tyrannosaurus Rex dinosaurs into the open plains so that they can eat all the little animals. The Surf_Aces can't resist this and while they're away we take the tiger. Weeble, weeble, weeble,' little shake of the left leg and into the crowd stepped the brown Bug.

'Brilliant! Great! That's one of the best yet!' cried Ram.

'Weeble, weeble, weeble,' cries filled the air. There was much left leg shaking as the word passed from Bug to Bug about this fantastic idea.

The noise was incredible. Eight million Bugs, 'Weeble, weeble, weeble,' at once, antennae swishing is quite a sound.

Ram and the Bugs, you'll notice, can be stimulated by the most simple and not even original idea. They like the mayhem and nonsense aspect.

Having DotCombo and the Surf_Aces fooled really good fun; they all enjoyed getting one up on DotCombo and any of her associates.

'Weeble, weeble, weeble,' another Bug stepped forward. This Bug was different. It had a hat on and glasses!

'Weeble, weeble, weeble, I'm a hip hop horrible Bug,' it said.

'Some folks call me "3H".' It smirked with a glint in its eyes. 'Let's release some of the Happy Virus into the web at the same time. DotCombo will have to split the Surf_Aces to deal with a variety of problems all happening at the same time. This'll gives us more time on the real attack to capture the tigers,' said 3H.

'Even better,' said Ram. '3H, I like your style, it's wicked,' said Ram. 'Why are you wearing a hat and glasses, 3H?' asked Ram. 'I've never seen anything like that before.'

'Weeble, weeble, weeble, I'm a hip hop horrible Bug,' said 3H, 'I'm a trendsetter and I can rap too!'

'Rap eh, well rap away,' said Ram.

The little Bug stood on the shoulders of some of his fellow Bugs.

Everyone could see him now.

I'm a hip hop horrible Bug, 3H is my name, watch my game, it sure isn't lame... don't, you like my style, hear me rappin' all the while, I'm walking the talk, I'm talking the walk, DotCombo and the Surf_Aces don't bother me I'm so evil my weeble weeble weeble is the biz, Take another look Surf_Aces take a look at thiz, With my weeble, weeble, weeble, my left leg a'shakin',

I'm a little terror in the makin', Lots of trouble, it's my game, I'm the hip hop horrible Bug, 3H, that's my name!

3H bowed, waved his hands in the air, shook his left leg and jumped back to the ground with his antennae swishing about from side to side.

'Weeble, weeble, weeble,' cries rang out all over the place. A huge ripple of noise rose up as millions of Bugs clapped and applauded their new star.

'Hey, you're the man,' said Ram. 'You're the man!'

'Weeble, weeble, weeble,' said the odd little rapping Bug, shook his left leg and disappeared into the crowd.

'Calm down everybody, the entertainment's over. We've got work to do. We'll create two diversions, one in the HistoryLand Disk and the other, as our little rapping friend 3H suggested, will be that we'll release the Happy Virus too. I think we'll set the Happy Virus off at all incoming e-mails, this'll cause a huge problem. Those Surf_Aces won't know where to go or what to do first, it'll be a real joy watching them sweat.' Ram burst into a loud long laugh. 'I sound like the Happy Virus!' he rasped.

Quickly gathering himself he coughed and said, 'I hate those Surf_Aces and as for DotCombo, she's the pits. Let's send them something to worry about!'

So the scene was set for a load of trouble on the internet. Ram decided that the attack would start at noon UK web time. An initial batch of the Happy Virus would be released at the first e-mails arriving onto the internet. Even the noise of them travelling about laughing and giggling would cause a problem for DotCombo and the Surf_Aces. A web hour later another batch would be released and each web hour after that until every e-mail was covered. As DotCombo sent for her Surf_Aces to deal with the Happy Virus, Ram would release intelligence that would alert Scanner to the HistoryLand Disk attack and the planned release of the dinosaurs.

'You know what you have to do!' he yelled at the Bugs. 'So get on with it!'

'Weeble, weeble, weeble,' shaking left legs, 'weeble, weeble weeble,' more shaking left legs and the Bugs were off over the horizon and into battle their antennae swishing.

Ram planned to co-ordinate the attack from his domain battle zone, which was in the cellar of the trash can area. In here he has a control desk with a battery of screens all showing the web and all the activities going on at any one time. Ram has links with the Bugs through their TV/voice ball and across the web he has visual contact using web cameras sighted at strategic points.

He will relay voice messages and pictures to the Bugs via the communication balls located on the top of their antennas.

His control desk was the very one he sat at when he was responsible for the internet, back in the days before he was banished. He rescued it from a recycling warehouse before it could be crushed. Its crushing was ordered by DotCombo. She wanted every last trace of

Ram removed but her order wasn't received in time and a horde of Bugs rescued it intact. Although it was of a lower standard than the state-of-the-art console DotCombo had, it was nonetheless very effective and served Ram well.

Really he didn't need a lot of flashy gimmicks or up to date toys or new inventions. He had plenty of tricks up his sleeve and, of course, his job was to make trouble, cause problems, disrupt and destroy. How he did it was irrelevant, it was the effect that mattered! The Bugs, who could be funny but also really bad, plus Ram's evil ways and superior intellect meant together they could create virtually anything they wanted with their innovations, inventions, ideas and access to all the old trash. Since nothing moved in or out of the web without their knowledge they were perfectly placed to construct and implement their variety of deeds without fear of being caught as no one dared to enter the domain.

Ram envisaged a glorious and complete wipe-out of the internet one day.

Oh, how he longed for this day! But first DotCombo, that useless little operative Click, sneaky Scanner and the Surf_Aces would need to be eliminated.

'The internet will be mine, it will be all mine,' he muttered under his breath.

'Weeble, weeble, weeble, it's noon, weeble, weeble, weeble,' came the message from the Bugs. 'Happy Virus ready to release, weeble weeble

weeble, sixteen e-mails coming in, twenty-five trying to get out, Superhighway loaded with dozens more.'

'Let's go,' commanded Ram in his sternest and deepest voice. 'Release the Happy Virus.'

'Weeble, weeble, weeble, here it goes.' A rush of laughter and giggles rang out across the web as the Happy Virus was released.

TROUBLE AND LAUGHTER ON THE WEB

DotCombo was sitting at her control module and didn't recognise the sounds at first. She thought it was noise coming from the Children's Zone, perhaps Kydo was telling more stories or playing games. She knew the Surf_Aces would be approaching the Animal Kingdom Disk having patrolled the Children's Zone for most of the morning.

'Click, are the Surf_Aces nearing the Animal Kingdom Disk?'

Click shuffled about pressing buttons and making clicking sounds.

'They're about ten minutes from the Disk, they've just passed the Guide to Italian Cooking Disk,' he called to DotCombo. 'Shall I signal them to advise exact and prime location, DotCombo?'

'No, if they're nearly on the scene have them confirm arrival when they are in the tracks of the Disk's readme compartment.'

Suddenly uncontrollable laughter jammed DotCombo's voice-activated headphone, the airwaves were full of the sounds of screaming e-mails.

'What's going on Click?'

'Looks like a release of the Happy Virus, DotCombo,' said Click.

'Scanner, did you know of this?' she called into her virtual monitor sound accessor.

'No,' responded Scanner. He was searching through the MusicLand Disk for some new sounds he could download into his personal MP3 player located on his Scandisk in a module embedded in the side of his visor.

Scanner liked the MusicLand Disk and spent most of his free time browsing there. Scanner could read the complete contents of any Disk without having to be absorbed into the tracks. It was this capability which earned him his reputation as the best browser and search engine on the web.

Icon and Scanner were both very up to date when it came to the latest trends in music. They were great friends and often spent time together discussing new ideas and musical tastes.

The MusicLand Disk was the place, thought Scanner, *it's where everyone who is anyone goes to see and be seen.*

The MusicLand is similar is the MovieLand Disk, thought Scanner, *except one has sounds and the other sounds and pictures!*

Scanner quickly dismissed this from his thoughts. Scanner had a big big problem on his robotic mind. *How could I have failed to pick up the release of the Happy Virus?*

DotCombo will go mad!

No one could outsmart Scanner. He knew and saw everything – or so he thought.

'I want answers!' shouted DotCombo into her

virtual monitor sound accessor. 'Scanner, is this real? Are we under attack from a batch of the Happy Virus?'

'Yes, my information indicates that the Bugs are after today's incoming and outgoing e-mails. I don't know why because they've never tried this before,' said Scanner, trying hard to cover his exposure with intelligent statements.

The Surf_Aces were now in the Animal Kingdom Disk, far enough away for the Happy Virus to cause extreme damage before they could return onto the internet to protect the e-mails.

'Scanner, get me a fix on what's happening. Scan the entire web!' cried DotCombo.

Scanner was really hot when he was in full scan-and-search mode.

This was Scanner's real asset.

'I'm getting pictures on my FPD (a flat panel display located on Scanners computer),' said Scanner.

He quickly uploaded these onto the Multiwall located in the central control module. 'It looks bad,' said Scanner.

'Click, get a signal to the Surf_Aces. I want to talk to them on the Visi-Tel,' said DotCombo.

The Visi-Tel is their credit card-sized sound and vision-emitting digital screen, a keypad which can pick up a two-way signal. It is attached by FLUG to each Surf_Ace. Some of the Surf_Aces wear the Visi-Tel in different places, some on their arms, others on their legs. Sometimes they wear it wherever they feel it looks cool!

The Happy Virus was running riot. It was now scattering across the internet. As each new e-mail moved through the internet, the Happy Virus would try to strike at the junctions or crossroads. This area is where the routing tables contain the software intelligence that dictates the correct destination address and makes sure that the e-mail is on the right course to reach its end-user. It's based on the radar beacon system used to guide aeroplanes around the world. As the plane passes between beacons it receives information on which course to take and how many degrees to turn through a series of instructions and directional data sent from the nearest radar station. The internet routing junctions perform the same task.

Ram could see the events unfolding from his control desk monitors.

Looked good so far, he thought. More e-mails were stacking up ready to come through the internet.

He liked the Happy Virus because it was very effective and, apart from all the noise, it was visibly spectacular.

The Bugs were having great fun.

'Weeble, weeble, weeble, look, look! An e-mail addressed to dotcombo@supanet.com, weeble weeble, weeble. Ram, an e-mail is coming through addressed to DotCombo!' the Bugs called excitedly.

This was more than Ram could have hoped for – an e-mail for DotCombo coming through the internet at the same time as the Happy Virus is on the rampage.

'Release more of the virus!' shouted Ram into his

command phone.

'Weeble, weeble, weeble, how much?' came the reply from the Bugs.

'As much as we have available, I don't want this attack to fail. I want to hit that DotCombo e-mail right where it hurts.'

'Weeble, weeble, weeble, we have enough virus to take out another eleven e-mails,' said the Bugs.

'What have we released so far and how many e-mails have died a happy death?' laughed Ram.

'Weeble, weeble, weeble, we released enough for twenty-three possible, we've had seven hits and more e-mails are coming through now.'

'Right,' said Ram. 'Release the lot, we can always make more. I want that DotCombo e-mail. Even if we don't get any others with this attack, this one will be more than enough.'

What a sight! The Happy Virus was now a real threat to the internet. Although it had been programmed this time to attack e-mails, would it only attack e-mails? No one could know, least of all Ram and the Bugs – but they didn't care anyway.

'Surf_Aces, DotCombo speaking from command module, over.' There was an air of urgency in her voice.

'Refresh here, DotCombo. We're locked on to you, over.'

'The Bugs have released the Happy Virus onto the internet. They're designed to attack e-mails if the intelligence Scanner has received from his search is accurate.' DotCombo sounded worried. She knew that unless they stopped this attack quickly, important e-mails of all types and sizes would be destroyed.

'Do you want us to return to base immediately?' asked Refresh.

'No, not yet. I need action. What are our options, comments please?' said DotCombo.

'It doesn't look like there is anything happening here in the Animal Kingdom Disk,' said Refresh. 'We could be back on base within 10 web minutes.'

'I don't understand why Ram and the Bugs would choose now to release their virus,' said Media. 'It's noon UK web time, what's the point? Ram knows that the busiest web time is early morning, as end-users switch on their PCs, and late at night as batch data files are downloaded. That's it,' said DotCombo. 'This has to be a diversion and a pretty bad one at that. Ram wants to tie us up with this Happy Virus menace while he springs another attack somewhere else,' DotCombo continued.

'Hey, you're on top form DotCombo,' said Refresh.

'But where will he strike if we're dealing with the virus?' asked Icon.

'That's anybody's guess right now,' said DotCombo.

'Scanner, what news do you have?' asked Tooltip.

'He's going to be banished to the periphery of the web along with Ram Router and the Bugs for missing this virus release; that's his news,' laughed Refresh.

'That's not funny, it's a cheap shot,' said Scanner.

'How could I have known they would release the Happy Virus today at noon UK web time? All the expertise available to me wouldn't have picked up this one.'

'You're a Scanner in need of a retune,' said DotCombo. 'I think your browser software isn't working properly. When this is over I'm going to have you upgraded.'

'Knockout!' exclaimed Scanner.

'Surf_Aces, we need to work quickly, we're wasting time now,' said DotCombo.

'I believe that an attack on the Animal Kingdom Disk will take place today,' said Scanner. 'Ram hit the charity web site again today,' he continued.

'Are you absolutely sure?' asked Refresh.

'Yes,' said Scanner confidently.

'Okay, let's go get the virus, sort it out and then come back here later,' said Icon.

'I would rather we split up and worked this one in pairs,' said Refresh.

'I agree, we need to split up. But before we run off in different directions, we need to know what we're planning to do when we reach the virus,' said DotCombo. 'If they're scattered all over the place we'll lose e-mails, that's for sure,' she continued. 'If we lose e-mails, we'll lose other data too and some of those messages will contain attachments.'

'I have an idea,' said Tooltip.

Tooltip always had ideas; some good, some terrific and some, well, let's just say some are better forgotten!

'He's the man,' said Scanner. 'He's the man!' Scanner continued sensing a Tooltip idea that would get him out of this jam and smooth over the embarrassing jolt to his reputation.

'We're not worried about what he is! Tell us your idea, Tooltip,' they all cried.

'I've been working on a new upgrade to our laser pod.

'Basically, at the moment we can fire our DBMs in bursts fairly accurately, but it's our skill, speed and movement that makes the weapon deadly.

'We know the Happy Virus is noisy. If we could programme the DBMs to lock on to this specific giggling, laughing noise, then fire our DBMs rapidly as we surf, move, twist and turn, we wouldn't have to be totally accurate. All we would have to do is lock on to the noise, fire and let the DBMs do the rest.'

'What an idea!' said DotCombo. 'I like it, but if it's not ready, what's the use?' she continued.

'I think the software I have is about ready and good enough for this,' said Tooltip. 'It's worth a try, we can refine it later if we have to.'

'Any other ideas?' asked DotCombo. 'If not, then we'll go with Tooltip's. Tooltip and Media you both return to the command module,' said DotCombo. 'We'll work on the re-programming the DBMs and you two will stop this virus. Refresh and Icon will stay in the Animal Kingdom Disk and wait further orders. But be alert, if Scanner is right then we're in for dual attacks. Let's all get to work, over and out,' said

DotCombo.

Tooltip and Media surfed off as commanded. 'DotCombo, an e-mail addressed to you is coming through the internet,' said Scanner. 'I can see the e-mail and a virus is heading towards the nearest junction and they're on a collision course!'

DotCombo called, 'Get me a full report, Scanner. I want to know what the e-mail is about, who it's from, its priority level, where it is at all times, where the virus is at all times, projected point, place and time of impact.

'Click, send a signal to Tooltip on his Visi-Tel and let him know what's happening. Give him all the details that Scanner gathers, ask him to head for this e-mail and take out the virus. He is not to return to base until he succeeds. He must not fail, that's an order. Tell Media to keep to her plan; we'll work on the DBMs with Tooltip on the remote. Maybe we could programme his DBM remotely too,' said DotCombo.

'What if none of this works,' said Click 'We could lose the e-mail and Tooltip too...' Click's words trailed away.

'It will be tough, but he won't fail,' said DotCombo smiling. 'Tooltip won't fail.'

'Weeble, weeble, weeble, we're laugh, laughing all the way!' shouted the Bugs. 'Weeble, weeble, weeble. Ram, all of the Happy Virus is now on the internet, weeble, weeble, weeble, DotCombo's e-mail is the next attack victim, weeble, weeble, weeble. The Happy Virus has it in its sights and what a lovely, lovely sight it is!' Eight million delirious Bugs were in raptures.

This is some day, a great, great day, mused Ram.

A Happy Virus loose on the internet, an e-mail for DotCombo at risk and an attack on the HistoryLand Disk to follow and then an all-out attack on the Animal Kingdom Disk to capture the tiger.

Ram hadn't experienced such an adrenaline rush since he took out the Spanish Galleon he'd found in the Famous War Battles of the Sea Disk last year. He couldn't forget the look on Lord Nelson's face when all of a sudden the ship the British fleet was attacking suddenly disappeared! Ram,and the Bugs had a special zapper which they used to hit web sites and for fun thought they would fire it during a visit to this Disk.

When they fired it, for some unknown reason the warship completely vanished. To this day Ram doesn't know where it went.

Oh, that was fun and exciting, thought Ram.

TOOLTIP AND SCANNER MEET THE HAPPY VIRUS

Scanner hadn't yet worked out all the various pieces of intelligence he now had arriving into his browser in bulk. It would be a few web hours before he had enough information to make a judgement and report to DotCombo. However, a key piece of intelligence was about to surprise Scanner in an unexpected manner and from a strange source.

Not for a long time had Ram felt so good, he was in control and the danger he had threatened for a long time was beginning to take shape.

'I bet DotCombo is worried, all her lovely little friends will be running around chasing their tails,' Ram called to the Bugs.

'Weeble, weeble, weeble, we're the busy Bugs, we're the ones who carry out the deeds of our great leader and we won't stop until we cause a jam. Oh great leader, we're your troops, we're loyal just to Ram!' they cried all in one breath into their antennae.

'I'm 3H, the hip hop horrible Bug. I'm back to rap for you, give it big licks, and use up all your tricks. Ram is the man, the Bugs go wham wham bam!'

It was the little brown Bug with hat and glasses. 'Weeble, weeble weeble,' a shake of the left leg and into the crowd he disappeared.

'The attack is on,' said Ram surveying the scene on his monitors. 'Viruses everywhere, go go go! I can't wait to see the e-mail heading for dotcombo@supanet.com die laughing.' Ram clapped his hands excitedly.

Meanwhile, DotCombo was now in full flow at her central control module. She revelled in co-ordinating, quickly assessing situations, making decisions and giving orders. She always listened and gathered information from all her sources, particularly the Surf_Aces and Scanner. DotCombo was always open to suggestions and on many occasions would override her own views and judgement for that of the group. She believed in individual brilliance, innovation, skill, capability and risk, but also in good team work and empowerment backed by excellent control and discipline. She also believed in the most important thing of all, fun and plenty of it. The Surf_Aces are bright, intelligent and friendly people who have a natural happy streak. But they also have a hard, ruthless edge when the internet is in danger. She trusted them totally. DotCombo would need her Surf_Aces at their very best if this current set of problems were to be overcome with the minimum of loss. This would require teamwork and at times individuality of the highest calibre.

The Happy Virus was everywhere, or so it seemed by the noise.

The cries of e-mails dying laughing was scary.

DotCombo called into her Visi-Tel, 'Surf_Aces get

ready for a long haul. Scanner, take a look around and see if you can pick up any new intelligence,' she said into her voice accessor.

'I'm getting conflicting signals, I just can't work it out,' called Scanner. 'I'm going for a browse,' he said sounding worried.

He wanted to take a look around the internet, he wanted to see the problem for himself. Scanner floated about propelled by a magnetic force similar to the Surf_Aces, boards and foot discs, but it wasn't as strong or powerful.

Meanwhile, Tooltip had arrived in the area where the DotCombo e-mail was supposed to be heading with the Happy Virus locked on to it. Tooltip couldn't yet see anything in his immediate vision, although he could hear screaming and laughing coming from all over the internet as the Happy Virus attacked the e-mails.

'DotCombo, over. It's Tooltip here,' he called into his Visi-Tel.

'Come in, Tooltip,' responded DotCombo.

'What's happening, any sign of my e-mail and the Happy Virus?' asked DotCombo.

'No sign of anything so far,' said Tooltip. 'Do you want me to take a scout around?'

'No better wait there just in case. We can't take any chances,' DotCombo replied.

Tooltip hovered at the routing junction keeping a close watch with his DBM primed and ready for action.

'DotCombo, come in, over,' said Tooltip.

'DotCombo here, what is it, has the attack started?' she said anxiously.

'No,' said Tooltip. 'Has Media arrived back at the control module?'

'She just got here no longer than a web minute ago,' said DotCombo.

'Good,' said Tooltip. 'Can we get started with the DBM sound lock on? I'd like to be ready as quickly as possible.'

'Yes let's go,' said DotCombo. 'Media, can you put Tooltip on the Visi-Tel and we'll work together.'

Media responded quickly, she was very smart and bright, always ready for action.

'Tooltip, what programme steps do we need to follow?' asked Media, now with Tooltip visible on the Visi-Tel.

'I'd like to make this a powerful weapon,' said DotCombo. 'I want to take this lot out, no messing,' she continued. 'I also want to scare Ram Router, he'll think we're beat on this one.'

'Right,' said Tooltip. 'Follow my instructions.'

Tooltip glided slowly about, ever mindful that suddenly he will have his hands full when the DotCombo e-mail and the Happy Virus arrive.

'Take the multimeter on DotCombo's console and slide it over to copy,' said Tooltip.

'Done,' said Media.

'Now put the DBM laser adjustment compact Disk into the DVD drive located in the PC on DotCombo's central control module,' continued Tooltip.

'Apply three virtual binary digits in the following sequence: 001011101101100001100101,' said Tooltip, 'and I hope I got that right, I took it from memory.'

'Done,' said Media. 'There's lights flashing and I've also got a flashing okay request on the screen, is this right?'

'I don't know, this never happened to me before, but if it's an okay question then move the cursor onto the box and click, we need to take the chance.' Tooltip was puzzled, he couldn't be sure that Media was doing everything accurately although he knew she was doing her best.

'Final move,' said Tooltip, still scanning the horizon for any sign of the e-mail or the Happy Virus. 'Last command input and if the right answer comes back, we're in business,' he said confidently. 'Key in exactly this sequence: 54287900235443278797l. Got it?' said Tooltip.

Media called back into the Visi-Tel, 'Can you repeat the last five digits Tooltip? Over.'

'Sure, they're eight... hold it!' he shouted.

'What is it?' called Media into her Visi-Tel.

'Tooltip, this is DotCombo, what's going on?'

'The Happy Virus and your e-mail are heading for each other!' cried Tooltip.

'I'd better go and meet them,' said Tooltip.

'The DBM programme – give us the last five digits quickly, Tooltip!' shouted Media.

'Can't wait,' said Tooltip, his voice fading as he sped

off towards the e-mail.

'Media,' said DotCombo, 'have you no idea what the last five digits were? Scanner, re-sequence the Visi-Tel recording. It's the only hope we have of rescuing the input from Tooltip.'

'I wasn't recording,' said Scanner, 'I'm out on the internet browsing for intelligence.'

'What!' called DotCombo. 'I want answers, Scanner, I want answers right now!' she blasted into her sound accessor.

'DotCombo, you didn't ask me to record,' said Scanner.

'Media, try to remember or we're in real trouble,' said DotCombo trying to regain her control.

'I'll try,' said Media, 'but I'm not sure. He said it very quickly.'

'Get him on his Visi-Tel,' commanded DotCombo.

'Tooltip over, Media here. Come in.'

'I'm with the e-mail and the Happy Virus is trying to catch it,' replied Tooltip.

'If I can lock on with my DBM and get a clean shot, I'll get the Happy Virus,' he said. 'It's squirming all over the place, can you hear it laughing?'

'Tooltip, we need the last five digits. Media can't remember them and Scanner wasn't recording!' called DotCombo.

As the DotCombo e-mail arrived at the routing junction the Happy Virus attacked. Tooltip decided he needed to get in between them if he was to get a clean hit on the Happy Virus.

Surfing, swerving and diving from side to side in an attempt to confuse and draw attention away from the e-mail, Tooltip surfed on a course that would put him in danger if he timed his move badly. Split timing movement was required and he decided to take his speed to eight quantum calamities and head straight for the routing junction.

Tooltip was just about there and about to shield the e-mail when suddenly the Happy Virus leapt in his direction and Tooltip collided with the Virus.

'It's on me!' cried Tooltip. 'It's locked onto me instead of the e-mail and is trying to wrap itself around me!'

Tooltip had the Happy Virus all over him. He quickly realised that unless he could free himself he was in serious trouble.

The Happy Virus was laughing and jumping up and down. Tooltip was doing the same; he had no choice, once the Happy Virus starts bouncing it's hard not to follow.

'Tooltip, please respond,' called DotCombo.

Tooltip tried to speak into his Visi-Tel, but it was hopeless. He was now crying with laughter as the virus started to affect his control.

'Ha, ha, ha, ha, hee, hee, hee, ha, ha, ha, ho, ho, ha, ha, hee, hee!' Tooltip was laughing so loud that although they couldn't see him on his Visi-Tel, they could certainly hear him.

'Tooltip,' shouted DotCombo. 'Tooltip!' she called again.

'The last five digits, I need the last five digits.'

'Try to shout them out as clearly as you can,' said Media.

'He, hee, heeee, ha, haaa, ha, ho, ho, hee, ha, eight, hee, hee, haa, ho, ho, ha, he, seven, ho, ho, ha, ha, nine,' poor Tooltip was now helpless with laughter.

'What came after seven?' shouted Media into her Visi-Tel.

'If we don't get this sorted I'll need to call in another Surf_Ace,' said DotCombo.

'I could go back and try to kill the Happy Virus,' suggested Media.

'You'll damage Tooltip,' said DotCombo. 'Remember the laser is just as dangerous on this Virus and will have the same effect as firing Gloob on a Surf_Ace,' said DotCombo. 'Anyway, I need you here to finish the programming once we get the last three numbers.'

'Tooltip, what comes after seven?' DotCombo was now shouting loudly.

'Ha, ha, ha, ha, he, he, ho, he, ha, he, ho, nine,' shouted Tooltip.

'Right, we've got two more to go, what are they Tooltip?' shouted DotCombo.

'Ho, ho, ho, he, ha, he, ha, ha, ho, ho, he, he, nine, ho, ho, he, he, ha,' cried Tooltip. Tooltip was losing his strength rapidly and was trying to stay alert; the laughing was making his sides extremely sore.

'Was that nine?' said Media.

'Ha, ha, nine, he, he, ho, yes, nine, ho, ho, he, ha,'

laughed Tooltip in pain.

'The last two digits, give us the last two digits Tooltip,' said DotCombo.

'Last two digits, he, he, he, ho, ho, ho, ha, ha, ha, last two digits, seven, ho, ho, he and one ha, he, ha,' at which point Tooltip collapsed.

'Got them,' said Media.

'Right, make the programme and run the test software,' said DotCombo.

'Once the test software is ready, load it into the DBM's memory and go save Tooltip. When you arrive, finish off the Happy Virus wrapped around Tooltip. He won't die, he'll just be very sore for a few days,' DotCombo said to reassure Media.

'But won't I kill him?' exclaimed Media.

'I'm sure Tooltip said the new programme was a different frequency that wouldn't harm a Surf_Ace,' said DotCombo. 'But you know Media, we won't know for certain until we fire it.' DotCombo was worried; this was a problem she hadn't expected to face. 'Look, let's be sensible. Tooltip would have said something; he's got the Happy Virus wrapped around him and he was giving us instructions for the DBMs,' she said as if trying to reassure herself that there was no danger to Tooltip himself.

'Right,' said DotCombo. 'Media, go kill the Happy Virus wrapped around Tooltip. Then re-programme his DBM and you can both go after the remaining Happy Virus still loose on the internet.'

'Got you,' said Media quickly heading for the

computer laboratory to run the test software.

'Refresh, come in, over,' called DotCombo into her sound accessor.

'Hear you, DotCombo,' responded Refresh.

'Tooltip's been caught by the Happy Virus and it's wrapped around him, he's laughing so much he's in tears.'

'Do you want me to go and get him?' said Refresh.

'No, Media has the data to produce the programme for the DBM sound lock on and she's going after Tooltip,' continued DotCombo. 'Refresh, you and Icon stay where you are, I'm worried about the Happy Virus and we still don't know where Ram and the Bugs will attack. Scanner thinks it will be the Animal Kingdom Disk but he's not sure, so he's gone browsing. If you two stay there then at least we're covered in case something should happen.'

'Okay DotCombo, I hear you,' said Refresh.

Meanwhile Scanner was on the internet. There was mayhem everywhere. The Happy Virus had been a success. E-mails lay dying, e-mails lay shaking and laughing uncontrollably. It was difficult not to laugh, the sound was infectious, but this was a serious problem Ram and the Bugs had unleashed – no doubt about that.

'Over here,' cried a small weak voice, 'over here, quick.'

Scanner searched around and there, lying flat, exhausted and almost dead, was a little e-mail. It was a birthday greeting, a singing webagram.

'I'm all laughed out,' it said quietly and very slowly. 'I was on my way to my routing address special birthday greeting when the Happy Virus appeared from nowhere. Once it had me at the routing junction I was trapped. I'm a goner, I know I'm not going to make it,' said the little e-mail.

'Look, I'm Scanner and my friends, the Surf_Aces, are working on a cure for this. Try and hold on for a bit longer,' said Scanner.

'I can't, I'm so weak. All the laughing is very strength sapping, I'm all limp,' it said.

'Hold on, come on you can do it!' urged Scanner. 'Look, just lie there, don't do or say anything.'

'I can't, it's too late for me, I know it, I'm fading away.'

The little e-mail was right. Once the Happy Virus attacked an e-mail there was no way back. A certain laughing death was unavoidable.

Scanner felt sorry for the little e-mail and tried to encourage it to hold on even though he knew it was really too late.

'Hey Scanner, want to hear my webagram birthday greeting?' said the little e-mail. 'Somebody should hear it before it's too late for me,' gasped the little e-mail.

'Sure,' replied Scanner.

'Here goes, then,' said the little e-mail leaning forward and opening slowly. 'Ahem, ahem, cough, cough,' the little e-mail cleared its throat and started singing quietly and softly.

Happy birthday to you,
Happy birthday to you,
Lemon barley for you,

Lovely sweets to chew,
Lots and lots of presents too,
A happy birthday on this special day for you,
Happy birthday, Master Dodger,
Happy birthday to you.

'Very nice,' said Scanner, thinking, *who makes up this stuff, it's awful*!

The little e-mail closed itself slowly and said, 'Here, listen. Come closer, Scanner.'

Scanner hovered across to where the little e-mail lay.

'You think this is the only attack, don't you?'

Scanner said, 'We think there will be another in the Animal Kingdom Disk, but we're not sure. Two of the Surf_Aces are on patrol there just now.'

'Come closer still,' said the little e-mail in a low whisper. 'There will be a diversion in the HistoryLand Disk at the same time as the Happy Virus action,' continued the little e-mail, fading fast. 'The Bugs are going to release the Tyrannosaurs Rex onto the plains, they'll eat all the little animals.'

'What!' exclaimed Scanner. 'How do you know this?' he asked.

'I heard the Happy Virus talking to a Bug just before it jumped on me.'

'They're going into the HistoryLand Disk, like I

said, and then there will be a big attack on the Animal Kingdom Disk.' The little e-mail was almost out of energy and slowly flopping over.

'What are they planning for the Animal Kingdom Disk?' asked Scanner.

'I don't know, something about capturing a T...' and suddenly the little e-mail was gone, another victim of the Happy Virus.

Scanner was upset. He'd never seen the result of a Happy Virus attack before. Poor little e-mail, what a shame and a webagram at that. Scanner also thought of Master Dodger who wouldn't get his birthday webagram e-mail and would be sad and disappointed.

Ram and the Bugs have to be stopped, thought Scanner. *We owe it to these little e-mails.*

Scanner realised his good fortune. The information he desperately needed had come from an unlikely source, the little e-mail.

What a star! he thought, *no time to waste now, I need to alert DotCombo.*

'DotCombo, can you hear me, over,' Scanner called into his visor. 'There will be three attacks. The Happy Virus is already underway, then the HistoryLand Disk and finally in the Animal Kingdom Disk.'

'Where did you get this from?' asked DotCombo.

'A little e-mail who has just laughed itself to death,' replied Scanner. 'It overheard a Happy Virus and some Bugs talking.'

'Excellent,' said DotCombo. 'Media, how are you getting on with the programming and the test software?'

'I think we're ready to try a sound lock on and firing,' said Media.

'Don't wait here, go to Tooltip and test it there,' said DotCombo. 'Scanner, organise a Visi-Tel conference hook-up. I want to speak to all the Surf_Aces, we've got some thinking to do.'

'I want the conference hook-up in 30 web minutes from now,' said DotCombo, striding over to her control module.

'Will do,' said Scanner, sensing relief that he had at last provided the intelligence needed which would go a long way to stopping Ram Router and the Bugs. His mind returned to the little e-mail without which he would never have guessed so quickly what was going to happen. Maybe his search engine would have eventually tapped into Ram and the Bug's activities, but a lot of time would have been wasted in the process.

He had a lot to thank the little e-mail for and Scanner knew it.

'I'm off to rescue Tooltip,' called Media into her Visi-Tel.

'Remember, conference in 30 web minutes,' said DotCombo.

'Refresh here, DotCombo, come in.'

'Refresh, any sign of activity?'

'Nothing yet. Icon has had a look about – but nothing. It's too quiet,' said Refresh.

'Scanner has information about the Happy Virus and another simultaneous attack on the HistoryLand

Disk both are a diversion. The real attack is on the Animal Kingdom Disk where you two are right now.'

'An attack on the HistoryLand Disk, where'd he get that one from?' enquired Icon.

'A little e-mail laughing to death told him it had overheard a conversation between a Happy Virus and one of the Bugs,' said DotCombo.

'Apparently Ram's plan is to create two diversions, one underway now, the Happy Virus, and the second in the HistoryLand Disk.

'The Bugs will release the Tyrannosaurus Rex on to the plains and they'll attack and eat the small animals. It's a frightening scenario. While this is going on, the real attack will take place in the Animal Kingdom Disk – but we don't know what that will be.'

'DotCombo, Icon here. I've put all my MusicLand downloaded music collection on the rare tiger.'

'How do you work out that one?' asked Refresh, a comment quickly supported by DotCombo.

'Well, it's obvious, nothing has changed in the Animal Kingdom Disk since DotCombo added the Indian elephants, remember?' said Icon. 'How long ago was that?' he added.

'Must be, what, two web years?' said Refresh.

'There you are then, if Ram and the Bugs had wanted to attack this Disk they would have found a reason long ago,' said Icon. 'We haven't had an attack on this Disk at all if my memory is right, correct, DotCombo?' added Icon.

'Wait, let me quickly run a scandisk check on the

memory files,' said DotCombo. 'Nothing. You're right Icon.'

'Hey, who's a clever Surf_Ace then?' said Icon. Shuffling his feet back and forth in a rhythmic movement on his surfboard, he did the splits and a double back somersault and landed upright with his arms folded across his chest.

'All right!' he yelled.

Icon learned this technique from Scanner who could waver and wobble about in time to the music. It looked cool!

Icon was trying to teach it to Kydo. He planned to take her to the web Garage music rave due in a couple of web months and she was keen to go.

'Icon, I know you're cool, but keep that for the rave,' said DotCombo. 'Maybe you can teach us all that neat little move when we've got nothing else to do.'

'Refresh, Icon, any more ideas? We're stretched to the limit,' said DotCombo. 'Tooltip is wrapped in a Happy Virus screaming his head off, Media is on her way to help him with the new sound lock on DBM.' DotCombo continued, 'Once she's rescued him, they'll both have their work cut out eliminating the remaining Happy Virus still on the internet.' She paused. 'Wait a web minute!' She sounded startled. 'What's that coming through on my Multiwall?'

'DotCombo, come in, over,' called Refresh and Icon.

'Well I never…' she continued.

'DotCombo, please. We're waiting,' said Refresh.

'Cache Downloader! It's only Cache Downloader, he's wandering across in the direction of the routing junction where Tooltip is wrapped up in Happy Virus, I'm sure it's him,' DotCombo sounded surprised but excited.

If it was Cache he couldn't have timed his entrance better.

'Scanner,' called DotCombo, 'I want better pictures of the routing junction where Tooltip is trapped. I want to see the image close up on the Multiwall.'

'It's Cache for sure,' said Scanner.

Scanner liked Cache; most of the web browser engines liked Cache. Well, after all, he did create most of them!

'Listen DotCombo, if it is Cache we could use him. We're short of bodies and Cache knows the web,' suggested Refresh.

'How about we ask Cache to work with Media to rescue Tooltip?' said Icon.

'Then what?' said DotCombo.

'Well, Cache has a traditional DBM, we could ask him to help us attack the Happy Virus with Media, then once Media's freed Tooltip he heads for the HistoryLand Disk and we'll deal with the main attack planned for here,' said Refresh. 'Media has the sound lock on DBM so she'll be able to work faster, with Cache on back-up it shouldn't take too long to finish the Happy Virus off.'

'Conference ready in 15 web minutes,' said

Scanner.

'All Surf_Aces stand by, except you Tooltip, for the moment, join us when you're free,' said DotCombo.

'Media, where are you? Is Tooltip in sight?' said DotCombo.

'Media, over. Yes I can see him, I'm going in,' she replied.

'Media, be careful. Remember the DBM hasn't done this before, so don't miss on your first shot. Refresh and Icon stand by, Visi-Tels to channel 439. Scanner, all vision on the Multiwall please.'

'Ho ho ho, he, he, ha, ha, oh my heavens, ho, ho, stop it, ha, ha, he, ha!'

Tooltip was lying on his back wriggling about, legs flapping and arms waving.

'Ho, ho, ha, he, ha, he, he, he, he!'

'Tooltip!' shouted Media. 'Tooltip, over here!'

Tooltip wriggled in the direction of the sound, he could see Media through the tears flowing from his eyes.

'Hurry up, ho, ho, ho, he, he, he, he, ha, ha!'

'Tooltip, I'm going to activate the sound lock-on on the DBM!' she shouted above the laughter.

'Ho, ho, ho, he, he, ha, ha, haa, haa, hhaauurrrryyy uppppppp, ho, ho, he, ha!'

Media took her DBM and pushed her hand through the magnetic strap, which held it to the palm of her hand.

'Here goes,' she said as she switched the sound lock on to ready.

'Haauurruurryyy upppppp,' shouted Tooltip. His strength was sapping, he was sore all over and losing energy fast.

'Sound lock on!' shouted Media. 'Sound lock on!' she shouted repeatedly and aimed the DBM directly at Tooltip.

A beam shot out of the DBM. At first it seemed to be off target then, as though realising its mistake, it wavered and shot straight at the Happy Virus wrapped around Tooltip.

A huge bright light burst in front of Tooltip and Media heard a high-pitched scream.

'Tooltip, you okay?' she cried. She couldn't see Tooltip because of the light and the flashing.

Suddenly into the air like a rocket flew the Happy Virus, screaming loudly. Like a shooting star it shot up and away, firstly out of sight and then it returned screaming and burst into flames beyond the routing junction.

'Tooltip, Tooltip where are you?' shouted Media.

'Over here,' he replied. 'I'm lying under the DotCombo e-mail, the blast blew me into it!'

'Hey, the sound lock on DBM worked!' Tooltip shouted excitedly. 'Didn't think I'd get to test it on myself, I was planning something different!' he said and almost laughed, stopping short and holding his sides.

'What a super weapon,' said Media. 'Listen, there's a conference shortly,' she said. 'Activate your Visi-Tel, Tooltip.'

'Okay,' he replied, dusting himself off and trying not to laugh.

The Happy Virus leaves an impression and it will take some time for Tooltip to recover. Another burst of laughter could be really sore and dangerous.

'DotCombo, over. Come in,' said Media, 'Tooltip is rescued and he's safe if a little shaken and sore after his laughing ordeal.'

'Welcome back Tooltip,' said DotCombo. 'Conference starts in 10 web minutes,' she continued.

'Media, Tooltip, we picked up what looked like pictures of Cache Downloader heading for the routing junction where you were trapped, any sign of him?'

'No, haven't seen him,' said Media.

'Maybe I was mistaken, it looked like Cache,' said DotCombo. 'I've asked Scanner to investigate and get us some clear pictures on the Multiwall. Let's wait and see,' she said. 'Media, programme Tooltip's DBM and you two get after the remaining Happy Virus as soon as this conference is finished, we'll not be long.'

'Tooltip let me plug my transfer cable into your DBM,' said Media. 'We'll need to act quickly, DotCombo wants the Happy Virus dealt with immediately.'

'Right,' said Tooltip. 'This is the second time you've come to my rescue, it's getting to be a habit!' he continued.

'Look Tooltip, if you can't look after yourself properly what do you expect?' said Media laughing.

'Don't make me laugh,' said Tooltip. 'Don't even

make me smile or I'll get out of control again.'

'What do you mean, get out of control again? You're always out of control!' said Media.

'Transfer starting,' said Media. 'How long should it take, Tooltip?' she asked.

'Roughly?' said Tooltip.

'Yes roughly,' replied Media.

'It's done,' he laughed. 'Oh no, oh no,' said Tooltip. 'Ho, ho, ho, ha, he, hee, hee, haaa, ho, hoo!'

'You're away again!' cried Media, trying not to laugh herself.

The after-effects of the Happy Virus could be very infectious.

'Tooltip, stop it!' she shouted. 'Calm down.'

'Media, what's going on out there?' asked DotCombo.

'It's Tooltip, DotCombo,' said Media. 'The Happy Virus is still in his system and he can't stop bursting into laughter. I'm laughing just watching him,' she giggled into her Visi-Tel.

'Fire your DBM at his feet,' shouted Refresh, cruising around in the Animal Kingdom Disk. 'That'll calm him down a touch!'

'Refresh, stop it,' said DotCombo. 'Tooltip!' shouted DotCombo, 'Get a hold of yourself.'

'Hoo, hoo, ha, ha, he, ha, he, he aarrghhh, aarrgghhh, ho, ho, ho, aaarrrggghhhh, my sides!' he cried painfully.

'I want the Happy Virus stopped and I want it stopped now,' said DotCombo, her voice, full of authority that Tooltip immediately stopped laughing.

'Right that's that sorted,' she said. *Nothing like a bit of good old DotCombo shouting to get everyone back on their toes*, she laughed to herself.

'Hey, you lot up there,' said a familiar voice.

'Cache? Is that you?' responded DotCombo.

'You bet,' said Cache speaking into his voice phone, an early version of the Visi-Tel.

'Welcome, welcome, it's been a long time,' said DotCombo.

'Surf_Aces, it's Cache Downloader!' cried Scanner excitedly.

'Good to hear your voice,' said DotCombo.

'Where have you been?' said Refresh into his Visi-Tel.

'Oh, here and there,' said Cache. 'You know me, always on the move looking for excitement and if possible a little danger, well, a lot of danger to be truthful.'

'Look Cache, give us a web minute,' said DotCombo.

'What's happening?' asked Cache. 'There's a lot of noise on the web, sounds like the Happy Virus is on the loose. Ram and his Bugs got you folks on the hop?' he chortled. 'If I can help, let me know, I'm heading for the Wild West Disk to see an old friend of mine.'

'Who's that?' asked DotCombo.

'Oh an old friend from the early days, Big Jake Badlands,' said Cache.

'Hey, I like Big Jake,' said Icon. 'He's cool and you

know what? He's got a new horse, it's wild, I think he calls it Meanstreet.'

'Tooltip, come in. DotCombo speaking.'

'Ready to go, DotCombo. The DBMs are primed and we can hear more Happy Virus sounds coming from the web where it rises to the east,' said Tooltip.

'Cache, good to hear you, but we've got work to do. Come on up to the central control module or go see Big Jake and I'll call you later,' said DotCombo.

'Listen, I'm not in a hurry,' said Cache. 'How about I help out Tooltip and Media? I fancy a pop at the Happy Virus,' he said.

'If you work with us you're under my command and control,' said DotCombo. 'You're not running about getting in the way, I don't have time for messing about.'

'Okay, okay,' said Cache.

'We could use his support,' said Tooltip. 'He's one of the best laser shots on the web.'

'Please DotCombo, I'll work with you but I'd like a little bit of free range,' said Cache.

'One step out of line and you'll answer to me. Remember you're an outcast and if you let us down you'll be back in front of me first and then GIZMA,' said DotCombo.

'I know, I know,' said Cache. 'Just a little action, please?' said Cache.

'First I want to talk with the Surf_Aces and then we'll decide what you can do, but only if we all agree,' said DotCombo. 'Tooltip, Media, go after the Happy

Virus. Don't waste any more time, you don't need to participate in the conference session now,' said DotCombo.

'Up and away,' said Tooltip.

'You sound like an early 1970s cartoon,' said Media laughing. 'Up and away sounds ridiculous, I'm sure you can come up with something better than that?' she called to Tooltip as they both glided, surfing and swerving across the web and away from the routing junction.

'Hey Cache!' shouted Media. 'Tooltip shouted up and away, that's one of your old phrases isn't it?'

'It's old all right, but I'm not that old,' said Cache as he watched them leave.

'How about "Surf_Aces Surfs Up"?' said Tooltip. 'I like the sound of that.'

'Bit too obvious,' said Media, swerving close to Tooltip.

Media was an excellent surfer. She could float, glide, swerve, and surf in all kinds of positions. Her favourite was an upside down move that she could hold for about a web minute. It looked spectacular and she enjoyed surfing.

'How about, out of the eye here come the Surf_Aces?' she suggested.

'What eye?' said Tooltip, almost hitting an e-mail, which had died another slow death at the hands of the Happy Virus.

'The eye of the wave, you know, in the surfing competitions they had to surf through the eye of the wave,' said Media.

'I don't like it, it's not catchy enough,' said Tooltip, priming his DBM for action.

'I bet Icon could come up with something. What's the phrase he uses, "cool"?' said Media.

'Yes, cool,' replied Tooltip.

'Watch it,' Media called, 'there's a Happy Virus and look, there's more over there.'

'Right Media, we'll go in swerving, gliding back and forth, I don't want them locked onto us so be careful. Make sure you don't give them a target,' he continued.

Cries of laughter rang out across this section of the web as dozens of e-mails lay, stood, sat and jumped about in fits unable to control themselves.

'It's awful,' said Media. 'Look over there at those e-mails, they didn't have a chance.'

'You might think that laughing is fun but when you can't stop it gets really painful, especially if there's no cure,' said Tooltip. 'I should know,' he said stifling a laugh. 'Remember what you need to do Media, prime your DBM and don't worry about aiming directly at the Happy Virus. The sound lock on should do the rest.'

'Okay, here goes,' she said.

Happy Virus cries are noisy and as Media and Tooltip coasted towards them they had to hold their ears to stop the infuriating sound from annoying them.

'Go, go, go,' said Tooltip and he let off a blast from his DBM that darted out and headed towards a Happy Virus wrapped around an e-mail.

The beam twisted and turned as it locked onto its

target.

A bright flash, a scream and the Happy Virus disappeared instantly.

'Success,' shouted Tooltip. 'It's better than I thought. Fire at will now,' he said to Media.

They both let off rapid fire as they swerved and glided in and out of the e-mails.

'Look at that one,' called Media. 'It did a back flip and a somersault before it disappeared. Try one that's wrapped on an e-mail.'

Tooltip fired at an e-mail in the last stages of dying. The beam twisted, turned, and took a path, which at first didn't look as though it would be on course to hit the troubled e-mail.

Boosh! The Happy Virus flew screaming up into the air and promptly disappeared! The e-mail bounced up as though struck by a bolt of lightning, yipped several times and quickly sped off through the nearest routing junction in the direction of its end-user address.

'A cracker,' said Media.

'Right, now we know what it can do,' said Tooltip. 'Let's spread out and get them all, where you see an e-mail still alive hit it and destroy the Happy Virus. Take it out before they strike again if possible.'

The flashes from the DBMs rained out in the direction of the Happy Viruses remaining on the web. There was no escape. The Tooltip programme was an outstanding success.

Ram watched from his control desk as virus after

virus met an explosive end. Worst of all, the e-mails already hit were being rescued.

'Bugs!' Ram shouted.

'Weeble, weeble, weeble,' as seventeen million appeared.

'Boy, you lot breed like nothing I've seen before,' he exclaimed.

'We're losing, Happy Virus, the Surf_Aces have a new weapon which appears to be knocking them out easily,' said Ram in a depressed tone.

'We need the Happy Virus to work for a bit longer until we get into the HistoryLand Disk and set the Tyrannosaurus Rex loose. Then the Animal Kingdom Disk attack needs to happen quickly on the back of all this mayhem,' said Ram. 'You Bugs forgotten how this plan was supposed to work? I'm not a happy camper, I'm very angry,' he said banging his fist on his console. 'What do we do? I need the Happy Virus for at least another web hour,' he enquired.

'3H, are you here?' asked Ram in a loud voice.

Out from the crowd stepped 3H.

'Weeble, weeble, weeble I'm a hip hop horrible Bug, 3H is my name.'

'Wait! Wait!' said Ram. 'Your rapping days are numbered my little friend if you don't fix this and fast,' said Ram, grabbing 3H by his antennae and shaking him about vigorously.

'Weebleeeee, weebleeeee, weeeeeeeblleelleee, Rammmmm, Rammmmm!' 3H tried to speak, 'Sssstttoppp sssshhaakkiinngggg mmeeemmmee, weeblleee, weeeeble, weeeeebbbblleeeeeee!'

'I'll shake your little antennae off altogether,' shouted Ram. Steam was coming from his ears and his face was becoming redder by the web minute.

'You and your Happy Virus ploy could cost us the big attack,' said Ram.

'Hoooowww, hhowwww wwwaaasss I,I,I,I,I,I, tttttoooo kknnnoooowwww?' said 3H. 'Hooww wwwaaasss I,I,I,I,I, tttttooooo kkknnnoowww?'

Ram stopped shaking him.

'Weeble, weeble, weeble, how was I to know the Surf_Aces would find a solution to the Happy Virus? It seemed unstoppable,' said 3H breathing deeply and trying to catch his second wind. 'Weeble, weeble, weeble, we didn't design the Happy Virus to withstand their DBMs,' 3H said justifying his original suggestion.

'They must have come up with something pretty good. The Happy Virus is fast and once it's on, it's impossible to shake off,' said Ram. 'I know the Surf_Aces are good with their DBMs but not this good. It looks from here like a complete wipe-out.'

'Weeble, weeble, weeble. Ram, I don't think the Happy Virus was a flop,' said 3H.

'Oh, you don't,' said Ram. 'Well, what do you call a complete wipe-out? A major outstanding success we should post on the entire web site?'

'I can see it now, Ram Router and the Bugs latest web disaster, the Happy Virus, kills itself laughing! Our reputation will hit rock bottom!' he shouted as if to emphasis his point to all the Bugs gathered.

There was much, 'Weeble, weeble, weeble,' and left leg shaking.

'Weeble, weeble, weeble. Look Ram,' said 3H, interrupting Ram's speech. 'We couldn't have known the Surf_Aces would crack this one. It happened so quickly we couldn't counter attack.'

'Weeble, weeble, weeble. We have tied up two Surf_Aces and they're still out there, it's not over yet,' said 3H reassuringly. 'Weeble, weeble, weeble, don't take it too hard Ram, the Happy Virus is a good destroyer and maybe with some adjustments, we can make it laser proof. Weeble, weeble, weeble, I've got some ideas,' said 3H.

'Put it like that, 3H, you're right, but I'm disappointed. One more disaster and you're history,' said Ram. 'I wanted that DotCombo e-mail and we didn't get anywhere near it. Smarty pants Tooltip got in the way and, but for a magical moment or two while he wriggled about jumping up and down laughing, we couldn't get to the e-mail. I wanted to know what was in it and now we'll never know,' he snarled.

'Weeble, weeble, weeble, if the Happy Virus can keep going for another half an hour of web time,' said 3H, 'we can still start the Tyrannosaurus Rex diversion.'

'It had better work 3H and you lot had better make sure it does too!' exclaimed Ram.

'Look Ram, a little rap will make you feel better,' said 3H.

'If I don't like it, you're tied to a computer game for the rest of the web week,' said Ram. 'In fact, that old 1970s tennis game sounds good – I'll tie you to the puck and we can bat you back and forward whenever we feel like it,' said Ram, picking up a racket and waving it about wildly.

Millions of weeble, weeble, weeble and loud cheers rose up from the Bugs. They liked this punishment; they could take turns at hitting 3H!

'Now, if you still feel like rapping... go ahead,' smirked Ram.

3H whispered softly, 'Weeble, weeble, weeble, I'm 3H the little rapping hip hop horrible Bug, I'm here...'

'Speak up!' shouted Ram.

Weeble, weeble, weeble, I'm 3H the little
    rapping hip hop horrible Bug,
I'm here to rap for you,
Surf_Aces, Surf_Aces you can try but you won't
win,
The Bugs are best, we are the best,
Don't hide or we'll seek you out,
With our big pal Ram, we've got the clout
already, Winners!

3H, 'Weeble, weeble, weeble,' shook his left leg, weebled again and stepped back into the crowd.

'Knockout 3H,' said Ram. 'But it won't save you if you fail! I want the Tyrannosaurus Rex release to go ahead now, no more delays. Soon we will capture that tiger!'

A blue Bug stepped out from the crowd.

'Weeble, weeble, weeble, I've got an idea Ram,' it said.

'Who're you?' said Ram.

'Weeble, weeble, weeble, I'm Arthur.'

'Arthur?'

'Weeble, weeble, weeble, yes – Arthur.'

'Arthur,' said Ram again. 'No self-respecting Bug would be called Arthur!' he laughed.

'Weeble, weeble, weeble. Well Arthur it is,' said the blue Bug.

'Well I never,' said Ram. 'One minute we've got 3H rapping in his hat and glasses and now we've got an Arthur! This place is full of surprises!' said Ram, staring directly at Arthur.

ARTHUR'S WIND MACHINE

'Okay Arthur, what's your idea?' said Ram.

'Weeble, weeble, weeble, I have a wind machine that will blow the Surf_Aces off their magnetic boards. Once they're off and can't escape we Gloob them, capture them and bring them back here,' said Arthur.

'I've heard everything now,' said Ram sighing. 'A wind machine? You just point it and blow, I presume,' said Ram, shrugging his shoulders and fixing Arthur with a glare. 'Come off it,' he continued, 'how do you make sure it only blows wind at the Surf_Ace?'

'Weeble, weeble, weeble, easy,' said Arthur. 'It's got a large funnel on the front to give it direction.'

'Can you demo it now?' asked Ram.

'Weeble, weeble, weeble, yes, I have it here,' said Arthur, pulling a giant metal box from the crowd of Bugs.

There was muttering from the crowd, 'Weeble, weeble, weeble.'

'How do you point it, Arthur? It looks heavy,' said Ram.

'Weeble, weeble, weeble, it requires 3.5 million Bugs to mould into a transporter vehicle so that we can move it around the web,' he said. 'Another 6.2 million Bugs will need to become a trajectory pod for aiming and firing.'

'How do you fire wind?' asked Ram. 'This is ridiculous, are you sane?'

'Weeble, weeble, weeble, I am completely with all my faculties!' retorted Arthur. 'Weeble, weeble, weeble, we don't actually fire it, but the routine is the same.'

'Fire it then,' commanded Ram. 'Fire it and let's see how powerful and accurate it is. Let's put the wind up the Surf_Aces!' He laughed.

'Weeble, weeble, weeble, I need 3.5 million of you Bugs to mould into a transporter,' said Arthur.

'Weeble, weeble, weeble,' noises and left leg shaking as 3.5 million Bugs moved around hurriedly.

Soon a giant trajectory pod appeared as the Bugs moulded their bodies into a single contraption. What a sight, it was enormous!

'Right Bugs, pull the wind machine onto the transporter,' said Arthur.

The machine was strange, it was a square box which looked round!

It was a kind of yellow and grey colour with little wheels made from computer hard Disks with tiny spokes, that turned as it was pushed onto the transporter. The funnel at the front was made from old computer monitor tubes placed one on top of the other. These were held together with a type of sticky tape that Arthur had invented himself.

'This is a monster invention!' said Ram, impressed by the ingenuity.

'Weeble, weeble, weeble, what do you want me to

aim at?' asked Arthur. 'We're ready to fire the wind.'

'I've never liked that mountain of old programme paper over there,' Ram said, pointing to a mound about three web kilometres high behind where the Bugs played on their chutes and swings. 'Fire at that,' said Ram.

'Weeble, weeble, weeble, copy that,' said Arthur.

'Copy that? What's this Bug talking about?' exclaimed Ram.

Arthur pointed his wind machine in the direction of the paper mound.

'Weeble, weeble, weeble, when I shout fire you 6.2 million Bugs over there make a trajectory pod!' called Arthur in a commanding voice.

'Weeble, weeble, weeble!' shouted millions of Bugs.

'I wish you lot wouldn't do that,' said Ram. 'It's far too noisy.'

'Weeble, weeble, weeble, get ready and on my instruction,' said Arthur, 'weeble, weeble, weeble, fire!'

The sound was huge as the machine burst into life whirring and puffing, it seemed to have a life of its own as it shuddered, juddered and banged up and down.

'What's it doing?' called Ram.

'Weeble, weeble, weeble, it's gathering wind prior to firing,' said Arthur, running about supervising.

Suddenly the machine took what appeared to be a long deep breath as if it were sucking in air!

Whooosh! Whoosh! Whoosh! A great blast of continuous air splurted from the front of the funnel.

'Weeble, weeble, weeble, aaaahhhhhhh, oooooohhhhhhhh!' the Bugs exclaimed.

'What a noise and the rush of air is phenomenal,' said Ram and punched his fist into the air. 'Yahoo!' he shouted.

The wind crossed the domain at high speed, heading straight, or so it seemed, for the paper mountain. All eyes were on the air as it passed.

It was an awesome sight and the sound was incredible.

'I didn't know wind could be like that, so fast, so powerful,' said Ram, who had a good view from his control console. 'This could be a winner, Arthur.'

The air rushed to the paper mountain and with a great crash it splattered paper everywhere and a loud boom was heard which reverberated around the whole domain. Paper flew in all directions, upwards, sideways, backwards, and in fact everywhere! The domain was covered from top to bottom. The blast had been so severe that it had shredded everything in the mountain and paper rained down like confetti. It was a delightful sight, what a mess! But that wasn't the end. The blast of air after disposing of the paper mountain, surged towards the back wall, bounced off, did a U-turn and headed back towards the command area where Ram and the millions of Bugs stood cheering.

'Weeble, weeble, weeble, watch out!' cried a horde of Bugs.

Too late. The air struck Ram's control console full

frontal, knocking Ram backwards, and also upwards.

'Heeeelpppp!' he cried as he flew backwards and upwards.

The force was so hard that not only Ram, but also around 4 million Bugs who had been standing beside Ram went hurtling in the same direction. Their timing couldn't have been poorer. The force of the air took them across the domain and straight towards a pond of new Gloob, freshly made that very morning.

'The Gloob,' cried Ram. 'The Gloob, the Gloob!'

Splash!

Too late, Ram and the millions of Bugs were covered in Gloob!

'Arthur!' shouted Ram. 'Arthur!'

'Weeble, weeble, weeble, here I am Ram, are you okay?'

'Oh yes, I'm okay,' said Ram sarcastically. 'Best bath I've ever had.' And he tumbled backwards into the Gloob.

The paper confetti continued to pour down, covering Ram and the Bugs. As it stuck to the Gloob they began to resemble animated paper monsters as they shook and moved up and down.

'Quick, get me the antidote. Get this stuff off of me,' Ram called.

'Weeble, weeble, weeble, what antidote?' called back the Bugs. 'Weeble, weeble, weeble, it hasn't been invented yet!'

'You telling me I'm stuck here?' asked Ram beginning to set fast.

'Weeble, weeble, weeble, you're stuck Ram,' said the Bugs.

'Weeble, weeble, weeble. Wait, I've an idea,' said Arthur.

'Arthur, if it's as good as your last one, don't tell me. Keep it to yourself,' said Ram.

'Weeble, weeble, weeble, no really. I could fire up the air machine again and blast the paper and the Gloob off all of you in one giant burst, weeble, weeble, weeble.'

'Yeah and blast us all to smithereens,' said Ram.

'Weeble, weeble, weeble, I'm serious,' said Arthur.

'So am I,' said Ram. 'You're not doing it!'

'Weeble, weeble, weeble, I'll put it on slightly more than half power, it should work just as well,' said Arthur enthusiastically.

'Have we any choice, has anyone got any brighter ideas?' said Ram, now rooted to the spot as the Gloob hardened faster.

Millions of Bugs were seizing up too and the situation looked bleak as Ram and the Bugs formed into a large mass of Gloob.

'One mistake, Arthur, and I'll come after you until the day I die,' said Ram.

'Weeble, weeble, weeble. Bugs, point the transporter at the pond of Gloob!' called Arthur. 'Prepare to fire from the trajectory pod.'

The air machine was turned round; with great care and attention it was pointed towards the pond of Gloob where Ram and millions of Bugs were trapped.

'Weeble, weeble, weeble, fire!' shouted Arthur.

Whooooosh! A loud rush of air was heard as it spurted out of the funnel.

'This had better be on half power,' said Ram.

But it was too late.

The air hit them with the force of a thousand hurricanes!

Ram and the Bugs were thrown back into the Gloob. Then, as the air rushed past, they were thrown out, and up towards the top of the domain.

As the air splashed past them, it took the Gloob and the confetti with it, much to the relief of Arthur and Ram. The pile of Gloob and confetti was pushed right to the roof of the domain where it promptly stuck, making a loud splat. It looked like a giant gooey paper chandelier.

However, although the Gloob had been removed from Ram and the Bugs one point had been missed when the plan was developed.

What would happen once the Gloob and confetti had been blown off Ram and the Bugs and they then started to fall back towards the ground?

Ram worked this out when he started falling back with no means of support.

'Arthur, what now?' shouted Ram as he hurtled backwards, the ground rushing towards him at speed.

'Weeble, weeble, weeble. Bugs form a giant net!' shouted Arthur.

The Bugs, never slow to react, made the largest and springiest net you've ever seen. It was huge!

Ram and the Bugs who had been propelled with

him were now in fast descent.

Looking down Ram called, 'Oh no, look out, here it comes again!'

They tumbled faster and faster gaining speed as they headed towards the giant net. But they didn't realise that the air was coming backwards too!

As Ram and the Bugs headed for the net, the millions of Bugs on the ground moved backwards and forwards, from side to side, tracking Ram and the flying Bugs as they fell towards them.

'Weeble, weeble, weeble, back a bit, left a bit, right a bit, left a bit, stay, no right a bit, stop!' called Arthur as he guided the giant net about the domain.

Ram was almost upon them now and he took up the gliding position used by skydivers. 'Stay there, don't move!' he called.

'Weeble, weeble, weeble, stand fast, hold tight,' said Arthur.

Just as Ram and the Bugs were almost in the net, the air rushed past them, turning them upside down and sending them all over the place.

'What the...?' said Ram as he somersaulted and spun in ever decreasing circles.

'Weeble, weeble, weeble, quick left a bit, left a bit, stop, no left a bit, left a bit, stop, no go, right a bit, left, left, left, right a bit, left, left, stop, stop, right, stop, stay. Stop. Stop. Stop. Stop. Stop!' shouted Arthur at the top of his voice.

The giant net of Bugs shuddered to a halt. All eyes were on Ram.

Ram, the bugs and a wind machine

Ram now completely upside down hurtled into the net followed by millions of Bugs. The dent was so large as they pushed down into the net that the kickback propelled them all, screaming and yelling, back-upwards.

'Waaaaaaaaa!' shouted Ram.

'Weeeeeeble, weeeeeeeeble, weeeeeeeeeeeble!' shouted the millions of Bugs.

Crashing back to the net again they bounced up and down like peas being tossed in a hot pan. The air by this time had blasted back into the roof of the domain. Although it was now rushing backwards it wasn't strong enough to cause any further damage.

Wyoong, wyooong, wyoong, wyoong, wyoong went the net as Ram and the Bugs bounced up and down.

Happy to be back on safe and firm ground again, Ram reeled on Arthur.

'Air machine, blast the Surf_Aces off their boards, eh? I'll give you air machine!'

'Weeble, weeble, weeble, it did work though,' said Arthur.

'It worked, but it was out of control and the side effects were not mentioned by you in your opening speech,' retorted Ram. 'Good try, but keep your ideas to yourself in future. They are too dangerous. Now, where were we?' asked Ram. 'Yes, the Happy Virus, not doing too well and an attack planned,' he continued, dusting himself down and scraping and pulling Gloob off his clothes.

'You know what to do, get to it!'

'Weeble, weeble, weeble,' cries filled the air as the Bugs rushed towards the exit.

'Conference is starting now,' said DotCombo. 'Visi-Tels to channel 439 and holding, pacer signals on active,' she continued. 'Scanner, a summary of what we know please for everyone's benefit.'

Scanner buzzed about officially, his movements making a skimming sound as the upward draft from his base pushed little currents of air around him.

'First Tooltip and Media are dealing with the remaining Happy Virus out on the internet with the new improved sound lock on DBMs,' said Scanner in a loud authoritative voice.

'I spoke to Tooltip about three web minutes ago and he reckons there are about seven Happy Virus left to kill,' said Scanner. 'Media thinks the new DBM will be a great weapon if we can lock it on to specific sounds, not just the noise of the Happy Virus.'

'We'll take a look at this suggestion once we've dealt with all the danger on the web,' said DotCombo. 'Scanner, continue. We don't have much time,' she said.

'Secondly, according to the little e-mail who died laughing, Ram and the Bugs plan to release Tyrannosaurus Rex dinosaurs into the open plains on the HistoryLand Disk so they'll eat all the little animals. It's supposed to be a diversion, like they don't actually plan to do it, only to make us think they're doing it, if you know what I mean,' said Scanner.

'You mean they plan on implied diversion?' said

Refresh.

'Yes,' said Scanner. 'The idea is we will react and send Surf_Aces to deal with the problem. This is designed to stretch us further on the assumption that we would still be fighting the Happy Virus. I know Ram is aware that the Happy Virus attack hasn't been completely effective. He's been ranting and raving up in the domain! Ram doesn't know about Tooltip's new DBM; he thinks the Happy Virus was a failure because Tooltip and Media were too good, which of course they were anyway! We still need Tooltip and Media to complete their assignment and finish off the Happy Virus. However,' continued Scanner whizzing about the central control area, 'the little e-mail who died of laughing said the real attack would be on the Animal Kingdom Disk and that the Bugs planned to capture something beginning with "T" – whatever a "T" is. There you have it,' said Scanner. 'In complete summary; Happy Virus being dealt with, Tooltip and Media on site, potential maybe/could be a Tyrannosaurus Rex escape and an attack to capture something beginning with "T".'

'Thanks Scanner, very interesting,' said DotCombo.

'I think they will release the Tyrannosaurus Rex because the Happy Virus appeared to be a failure,' said Icon. 'It's what I would do if I wanted to get even.'

'You know Ram,' said Refresh. 'He's spiteful and will be hurting. I agree with Icon.'

'Let's assume you're both correct,' said DotCombo. 'How should we react?'

'I suggest that Icon and myself remain here in the Animal Kingdom Disk, if Ram is going to do something it will be soon,' said Refresh.

'What about the something beginning with "T", any ideas on that one?' asked DotCombo.

'Yes,' replied Refresh. 'I agree with what Icon said earlier, it's got to be the rare breed of tiger you put in the Disk recently. What else do we know starts with a "T" that Ram would want?'

'Talligator!' laughed Scanner.

'Thanks Scanner,' said DotCombo. 'Nice to see you've still got your sense of humour.'

'It's the tiger for sure. I'm convinced Ram would want to get hold of something he could trade,' said Refresh. 'I think he'll release the Tyrannosaurus Rex to cause havoc and at the same time take the tiger – so we should stay here,' said Refresh.

'I think we're all agreed on what we think he'll do, but I assume you're suggesting that we send Tooltip and Media to deal with Tyrannosaurus Rex?' said DotCombo.

'Why not?' said Icon. 'They should be finished soon and could head to the Disk immediately. I think both Refresh and I will have our hands full when the Bugs come to take the tigers. The Tyrannosaurus Rex will need two Surf_Aces to put them back into their compound before they cause too much damage,' he continued.

'What if some of the Happy Virus are still loose?' said Scanner. 'Could we send Tooltip to the

Tyrannosaurus Rex problem and leave Media to finish the job?'

'Tooltip, come in,' said DotCombo into her voice accessor.

'Tooltip here, DotCombo,' replied Tooltip.

'How much more time do you need to finish off the Happy Virus?'

'We've got about three or four to go although there could be some out on the edges either hiding or about to strike – you know, some stragglers,' said Tooltip. 'The DBMs are doing a great job. Media has taken out five at the same time with a couple of bursts of the laser, the sound lock on is working better than I had planned.'

'Do you think you'll be finished in about ten web minutes?' said DotCombo.

'Should think so, although I would need to make sure there are no more of the Happy Virus hiding or whatever,' responded Tooltip.

'Can you deal with the Tyrannosaurus Rex problem with Media, Tooltip?' said DotCombo.

'If it can wait 10 to 15 web minutes, sure we'll go,' said Tooltip.

'Have we got 10 to 15 web minutes?' interrupted Refresh.

'Surf_Aces, I just don't know!' said DotCombo.

'I don't think we do,' said Icon.

'I'll second that,' said Scanner.

'Ram and the Bugs will need to act soon or the momentum will be lost. If he is trying to split us, he needs to do it now,' said Refresh.

'DotCombo, come in. Over,' said Tooltip.

'What is it Tooltip?' she asked.

'I think they've released some more of the Happy Virus. I can hear loud noises and laughter at routing junction E46870,' said Tooltip.

'Great,' sighed DotCombo.

'That's Ram all right, he won't stop until he gets revenge,' said Refresh.

'Scanner, has there been another release?' asked DotCombo.

'Yes,' replied Scanner. 'DotCombo, your e-mail has just arrived safely,' he continued.

'Thanks to Tooltip it made it,' said DotCombo. 'Bravo Surf_Aces!' she cried.

'What does it say, DotCombo?' asked Refresh.

'Wait, I'm opening my mail,' she said. 'Well, would you believe it, it's a message from GIZMA.' She read it and said, 'Listen to this and I quote: DotCombo, expect a release of the Happy Virus by Ram Router and the Bugs at noon UK web time, have all Surf_Aces on full alert, quantities unknown at this time. Best regards, GIZMA.'

'Boy, do these guys know how to keep hot information on the move. Good old GIZMA, right on the ball again!' she said sarcastically. 'Can't they use the Multiwall and send a visual instead of an e-mail if it's so urgent, knowing there's a Happy Virus on the rampage?' she rasped.

'I wouldn't be too hard on them DotCombo, they

mean well. After all, we rely on Scanner for most of our intelligence,' said Refresh.

'You're right Refresh, I'm just angry, everything seems to be boiling and we're at sixes and sevens about what to do about it,' she said, her voice filled with frustration.

'DotCombo, have to go quickly. There are dozens of the Happy Virus at routing junction E46870,' said Tooltip into his Visi-Tel.

'Tooltip, can you handle it by yourself?' enquired DotCombo.

'No, we can't be sure exactly how many there are, I don't want a repeat of this morning,' said Tooltip, his voice overflowing with urgency. 'We need to go DotCombo, there's e-mails out there coming in both directions.'

'Tooltip, Media, DotCombo here again. You've got one web hour and then you call for further orders, I still might need you to go to the Tyrannosaurus Rex problem. Time is short.'

'Hey gang, just when you thought I'd gone off to see Big Jake Badlands I'm back again. I didn't go, too much going on here and I wanted to take a peek,' said Cache.

'Cache, where exactly are you?' asked DotCombo.

'I'm just passing routing junction B433250123, I'm roughly about 8.23 web minutes from your base,' said Cache.

'Cache, you just wait there,' said DotCombo.

'Scanner, pick up a Visi-Tel and head for Cache.

Quickly, I want to speak to him and talk over an idea I've just had.'

'DotCombo, Refresh here. Are you thinking what I'm thinking?'

'Could be, Refresh,' replied DotCombo. 'Cache could deal with the Tyrannosaurus Rex, he owes us a favour and with the right briefing and equipment, why not?' said DotCombo.

'Can we have Scanner take a DBM with him too, just in case Cache doesn't have anything as powerful,' said Icon.

'Good idea, Icon,' said DotCombo. 'Scanner, take a DBM too.'

'Cache, DotCombo here. I could use a favour, are you up for some excitement?'

'You bet, DotCombo. Ready and willing,' said Cache.

'Scanner is on his way to meet you, so don't move,' said DotCombo. 'He'll bring a Visi-Tel and a DBM.'

'What's the problem?' asked Cache.

'Let's just say we've got several and I want you to handle one of them,' said DotCombo. 'Ram and the Bugs have released the Happy Virus onto the internet. Tooltip and Media are dealing with it but they seem to be releasing more, it will take some time to finish them off completely,' said DotCombo.

'Not only that, but they plan to enter the HistoryLand Disk and release Tyrannosaurus Rex onto the plains to eat all the little animals,' she continued.

'Wow!' said Cache. 'Our Ram Router has been

busy.'

'He's been busy all right,' said DotCombo. 'At the same time he plans to attack the Animal Kingdom Disk and capture the rare tiger!'

'DotCombo, what can I do to help?' asked Cache.

'Well Cache, I need Refresh and Icon to stay in the Animal Kingdom Disk, the Bugs should arrive soon and we'll need to be vigilant. Tooltip and Media are working on the Happy Virus. I can't afford to split up the Surf_Aces any further. All of these situations are extremely dangerous and time consuming and that's where you come in,' she continued. 'Cache could you handle the Tyrannosaurus Rex problem alone? It might be a false alarm, but then again it might not,' said DotCombo. 'Take Scanner if you want, he could search out the Tyrannosaurus Rex,' said DotCombo.

'Deal,' said Cache. 'I'll take Scanner too.'

'Thanks Cache, when Scanner arrives with your Visi-Tel and DBM, head for the Disk with him, call in when he arrives and I'll give you further instructions,' said DotCombo.

'Okay DotCombo, good to be working with you again. Perhaps when this is all over we can go out...' said Cache.

'Just hold it there,' said DotCombo. 'Business first and then maybe we'll think about going out,' DotCombo rounded on him quickly. 'You want this job Cache, you stick to the task in hand and that's final!'

'Hey Dorothy,' said Cache.

'DotCombo to you, Cache Downloader, and don't you forget it!'

'Refresh,' said DotCombo, 'did you pick up this conversation with Cache?'

'Yes DotCombo, both Icon and I stayed online. We know what you're trying to do, good idea too, old Cache working for DotCombo and the Surf_Aces, like it, it's neat!'

'Right, everyone know what they're doing?' said DotCombo.

'Yes,' said Refresh.

'Yes,' said Icon.

'Yes, we're on site and firing at random, the Happy Virus is everywhere,' said Tooltip.

'I reckon there's about fifty to sixty out here,' said Media. 'Good luck to Cache.'

'Cache, is Scanner there yet?' asked DotCombo.

'No sign yet Doroth... sorry – DotCombo. I'll let you know as soon as he arrives,' said Cache.

'Scanner, where are you?' asked DotCombo.

'I'm about 11 web minutes from Cache,' said Scanner.

'Good luck, everyone, do your best and please keep in touch. I want updates every web minute. Scanner, keep your browser running,' said DotCombo. 'Click, more orange juice please.'

'Right away,' replied Click, click clicking switches and pressing buttons.

'Bugs!' shouted Ram.

14.6 million Bugs appeared.

'One of these days I'm going to shout "Bugs" and the place will overflow with you lot!' exclaimed Ram. 'I've called you here to review the situation,' said Ram.

'More of the Happy Virus has been released, well, all that we have left apparently. Tooltip and Media appear to have the upper hand. The attack in the HistoryLand Disk should start any minute, and then the tiger will be captured. I need ideas, we have to stay one step ahead should anything else go wrong,' said Ram twiddling his laser gun round his finger.

Suddenly a burst of laser light darted from the gun and a Bug screamed.

'Ooops,' said Ram. 'Didn't mean to do that, are you okay?'

'Aarrggh, yes I think so,' said a little beige-coloured Bug holding and rubbing its head. 'That hurt!'

'I get carried away sometimes,' interjected Ram, feeling sorry for the little beige Bug who was still rubbing his head.

Ram's sympathy didn't last long and soon he'd fixed his stare again.

'I want to maximise the damage and when we attack this time I want total success!'

Ram was not in the mood for failure and all the assembled Bugs understood this perfectly. They stood with their little left legs shaking and their antennae swishing back and forth.

THE DOTCOMBO VOICE SIMULATOR

'Weeble, weeble, weeble,' said a little yellow Bug who had stepped out from the crowd. It shook its left leg and said, 'Weeble, weeble, weeble I'm called Yellow because I'm coloured yellow and I have invented a DotCombo voice simulator.'

'Voice simulator?' said Ram, his eyes lighting up, as he stared at the little yellow Bug.

'How does it work, Yellow?'

'Weeble, weeble, weeble, the basic idea is it mimics DotCombo's voice,' said the little yellow Bug. 'Weeble, weeble, weeble you speak into this microphone and instead of Ram Router's voice, DotCombo's voice is heard instead! Weeble, weeble, weeble, if I speak into it,' said the little yellow Bug, 'weeble, weeble, weeble, my voice would sound like DotCombo's too.'

'Marvellous,' said Ram. 'What's it connected to? How will everyone hear me as DotCombo?'

'Weeble, weeble, weeble, it's attached to the Surf_Aces Visi-Tel sound system,' said little Yellow. 'Weeble, weeble, weeble, they'll hear every word loud and clear. Weeble, weeble, weeble, they'll hear every instruction and command as if it were DotCombo herself giving it,' smiled the little yellow Bug.

'Brilliant, can I try it?' said Ram.

'Weeble, weeble, weeble, sure,' said Yellow.

Ram pulled the device towards him, switched on the microphone, and spoke.

'Whheee, whaafftt, wotttttllle, whuffftt, splurgeeee, clumppp, smolffllfft doesn't sound like DotCombo to me,' said Ram with annoyance. 'I hope this isn't another glorious Bug failure. They're coming thick and fast at the moment!'

The little yellow Bug rushed over and quickly made some adjustments behind the console.

'Weeble, weeble, weeble, that should do it, the Lax Benicular Grobble lever wasn't switched on,' said the little yellow Bug.

'I'll switch on your Lax Benicular Grobble in a web minute,' said Ram.

'Weeble, weeble, weeble, try it again.'

Ram leaned forward and spoke into the microphone.

'Surf_Aces this is bleep, bloop, bleep, wheeeeee, bloop, clip, clap, dingle, dibble, bingle, this is your bloop, bleep, leader, barble, dingle, dot... frupple, com, bloop, bleep, wheeee, here. This is useless,' said Ram. 'I sound like a demented ferret!'

'Weeble, weeble, weeble, I don't understand it, I had it working this morning,' said the little yellow Bug. 'Weeble, weeble, weeble, one more adjustment, I think I know what's wrong.'

'Last chance saloon, Yellow,' said Ram growing impatient.

The little yellow Bug disappeared again behind the console and much banging and thumping was heard. Pieces of metal, bits of wood, cables and components flew from the back of the console. Suddenly there was a loud bang followed by a flash of smoke, the little Bug appeared in a cloud of black smoke and sparks covered in dust! He seemed to stagger and bounce about, electrical charges bursting from his body. His antennae were twisted and bent, little puffs of smoke were popping out at regular intervals.

'Weeble, weeble, weeble, cough, cough, cough, that's it, cough,' he said confidently.

'What was it this time?' said Ram. 'The Lax whatever it was Grobbling thingy again?' he asked sarcastically.

'Weeble, weeble, weeble, should have seen it earlier, the Crimble Cutter was loose and shorting the Analytical Wascome Filter,' said the little yellow, but now slightly black, Bug.

'You're making this up as you go along,' said Ram. 'You haven't a clue, Lax Benicular Grobbles and Analytical Wascome Filters. This is gibberish!' said Ram. 'This is your last shot, it had better work this time.'

'Weeble, weeble, weeble, try it now, Ram.'

'Right, connect me to the Surf_Aces Visi-Tel voice channel. Which one is it, 566?' said Ram.

'Weeble, weeble, weeble, it's 5699,' said the little yellow Bug with black markings.

Ram leaned forward again and spoke into the

microphone.

'This is DotCombo here. Surf_Aces, listen and be at attention!'

Putting his right hand across the microphone he exclaimed, 'It worked little Bug, it worked! We'll have some fun with this. I want to use it immediately. I'll send the Surf_Aces all over the place. Ha, ha, ha!' shouted Ram. He was pleased now and a large grin covered his face. 'Set it up so I can be heard on their Visi-Tel sound systems right away, Yellow.'

'Weeble, weeble, weeble, you've got it!' said the little Bug, beaming from cheek to cheek. In fact, all the millions of gathered Bugs were smiling.

Yellow set it up and stepped back into the crowd, left leg shaking and antennae swishing all over the place. It seemed to have a life of its own; clearly an electrical charge works in mysterious ways if you're a Bug! Puffs of smoke continued to pop from it as Yellow disappeared into the crowd.

There were enormous cheers from the assembled millions of Bugs.

'Weeble, weeble, weeble!' they shouted. 'Well done, Yellow!'

'Weeble, weeble, weeble, I've a rap for this,' said 3H stepping from the crowd, shaking his left leg and walking slightly off balance towards the console where Ram was sitting.

'3H, remember you're in the bad books, after the Happy Virus debacle this had better be good,' said Ram, pleased with his new toy and in no mood for failures.

Weeble, weeble, weeble, I'm the hip hop
   horrible Bug,
3H is my name,
I rap all day and rap all night,
It's me who raps, it's all night noise,
Making hip hop raps for all the girls and boys,
It's me who's the star, it's me who's so cool,
Go on Ram tune in the voice box,
Make those Surf_Aces look the fool.

'Electric,' said Ram. 'Now beat it! Get it?' he laughed.
'Beat it!'

Silence, not a sound, except for millions of feet
shuffling back and forth. The Bugs never ever
understood Ram's jokes.

'Suit yourselves, I liked it, it was a hip hop horrible
joke!'

'Weeble, weeble, weeble, oooohhhhh, beat it as in
rapping,' said the Bugs getting the joke at last. 'Weeble,
weeble, weeble, funny, very very funny.'

3H stepped back into the crowd, his left leg shaking
to thunderous applause.

'Weeble, weeble, weeble. Ready to go, Ram,' said
Yellow. 'Channel 5699 open.'

Ram flicked a large silver switch marked 'ON'.
Hundreds of lights burst into life and started flashing
in what appeared to be a totally random sequence.
There was weird whirring, crunching and grating
noises coming from the voice simulator. It shook
rapidly and vibrated across Ram's desk, stopping just
before it fell over and onto the floor below.

'This in the plan, Yellow?' said Ram. 'It's not going to explode or anything?'

'Weeble, weeble, weeble, perfectly okay, everything's working to specification,' said Yellow, still smouldering with little puffs of smoke spurting out of his bent antennae. 'Go ahead Ram, speak. It's okay, this'll work.'

Ram tried again.

'Surf_Aces, come in, DotCombo here. Surf_Aces are you there? Hello, hello, DotCombo calling, respond please.'

'Refresh here, DotCombo. What is it?'

Ram looked up and smiled a broad smile at the Bugs who all nodded in unison.

'Give me your exact position, Refresh,' continued Ram.

'I'm in the Animal Kingdom Disk with Icon, we're entering the African Jungle area and heading to where all the tigers have their afternoon siesta.'

'Refresh, go immediately to Beach Baby World Disk, there's an expected attack by Ram and the Bugs to re-programme the Disk and switch off the sun,' said Ram.

'What about the tigers?' enquired Refresh.

'Scanner now says it's a hoax, call off the search.'

'But the little e-mail overheard the Bugs talking,' said Icon.

'He was lying and he was out of control, all that laughing you know,' said Ram, having to think fast.

'Okay we're on our way,' said Refresh.

'Over, up, up and away and out!' said Ram as DotCombo.'

'It worked perfectly!' shouted Ram to the Bugs. 'We've got a winner here!'

'Weeble, weeble, weeble, it's a winner, it's a winner!' shouted the Bugs.

Refresh and Icon started their manoeuvre to leave the Animal Kingdom Disk. Icon glided from side to side, swirling in and out of trees and bushes whereas Refresh was more direct, making small turns and keeping close to the tracks.

'You know, Icon. I just don't understand, DotCombo was sure they would attack the Animal Kingdom Disk and take the rare tiger. I wonder where she got the hoax information from. Scanner, maybe?'

'What about the little e-mail story, surely it wasn't lying?' said Icon.

'Why would Ram want to switch off the sun in the Beach Baby World Disk. They know we'll not allow that to happen, the Beach Babies will freeze as it'll be permanent night-time. He wouldn't be that cruel, would he?' said Refresh, puzzled. 'I don't like it,' said Refresh. 'It doesn't sound like DotCombo, she would have asked for advice before sending us in a different direction. She wouldn't have just told us to go anywhere.'

They both hovered together talking and bouncing questions off each other.

'Icon, I want you to return to the central console and speak to DotCombo in person. No Visi-Tels, okay,' said Refresh.

'If you're wrong, Refresh, DotCombo will be angry, this could put the whole operation at risk, I mean, we're doubting her word,' said Icon.

'This is too serious, Icon. We have to take the risk. I'm worried that the message we were given didn't come from DotCombo,' said Refresh.

'What, well where did it come from?' said Icon.

'That's what we need to find out, off you go and keep all contact with me on scrambler channel 277 only until you are with DotCombo in person. If you're there when she speaks we'll know it's the real DotCombo for sure. I'm staying here in the Animal Kingdom Disk, I've got a funny feeling the Bugs will attack here soon.'

'Take care, Refresh. I'll call you soon,' said Icon, swerving sideways in a circle and then turning, waved at Refresh and sped off into the distance.

'Tooltip, Media, are you there? Come in,' said Ram, now warming to the part.

'Tooltip here, DotCombo.'

'I'm here too,' said Media.

'Forget the Happy Virus, now you've nearly finished them all off those left won't cause any more real problems even if they get an e-mail or two. I want you, Tooltip, to go to the Millennium Game Disk. Ram's planning to disrupt the game so everyone always loses. Scanner has just received a report from the Game Master.'

'Copy DotCombo, I'm on my way,' said Tooltip.

'Media, my little precious Surf_Ace, there's a problem at the Fashions Through the Millennium Disk. Ram plans to destroy all the clothes and we need to get there first.'

'I'm on my way, DotCombo. Over,' said Media.

'Who's a clever boy then?' said Ram as he stood to enjoy the adulation of his adoring Bugs who clapped, whistled and shook their left legs.

'The Surf_Aces are now split up and all over the place. The only one who could be a problem is Refresh, he's smart and he'll be wondering what's going on,' said Ram. 'Also where did Icon go? He's completely disappeared.'

'Weeble, weeble, weeble, I don't know,' said a grey Bug who stepped forward, shook his left leg and hiccuped twice before it stepped back into the crowd.

'You should get something for that,' said Ram. 'Like a blast from my laser gun. That would definitely cure the hiccups!'

'Weeble, weeble, weeble, why don't you call Icon and pretend to be DotCombo,' said Yellow stepping back out from the crowd.

'Good idea,' said Ram. 'Icon? DotCombo here, over.'

Silence.

'Icon? Please respond urgently, DotCombo here.'

'Refresh here, what is it DotCombo?'

'Ah Refresh, where is Icon? He should be with you but he's not responding, is his Visi-Tel working?' enquired Ram.

'He's in the deep jungle area. Contact is difficult in there because of all the trees, bushes and mountains. He'll be back in about a web half hour,' said Refresh, stalling for time.

'Make sure he calls in when he gets back!' barked Ram.

'I will,' said Refresh. 'Over.'

'Something's up,' said Ram. 'He's playing for time, what's he up to?'

'Weeble, weeble, weeble, maybe he's telling the truth,' said Yellow before stepping back into the crowd.

'Yeah, that's it,' said Ram, not entirely convinced. 'Listen up my merry little Bugs, we attack the Animal Kingdom Disk and capture the rare tiger in one web hour.

'At the same time, instead of an implied diversion for the HistoryLand Disk, I want to do it for real and release the Tyrannosaurus Rex onto the plains!' he shouted.

'Weeble, weeble, weeble!' shouted the Bugs. 'Weeble, weeble, weeble!'

'Weeble, weeble, weeble, I'm the hip hop horrible Bug 3H is my name…'

'We haven't got time for that, 3H, we've got work to do,' said Ram, cutting 3H off in mid rap.

'Refresh, give me an update,' said the real DotCombo.

'Refresh here, DotCombo. Still quiet.'

Refresh couldn't let DotCombo know what was

happening and that Icon was on his way back to the central module.

'Refresh, are you sure everything is okay? You don't sound very confident,' DotCombo enquired.

'It's hot in here and I'm thirsty,' replied Refresh.

'How's Icon?' asked DotCombo.

'He's okay, but hot too,' said Refresh.

'Icon? How are you?' asked DotCombo.

'He's just gone down to the lake to where there's a breeze,' interrupted Refresh. 'His Visi-Tel's here with me.'

'You know I don't like the Visi-Tel to be removed from a Surf_Ace unless it's a life or death situation!' said DotCombo.

'I know, DotCombo,' said Refresh as he struggled to find a suitable excuse. 'It won't happen again, I'll talk to him when he gets back,' said Refresh.

'Make sure you do, Refresh. I'm holding you responsible, you should know better. Keep me informed the moment anything stirs, over and out,' said DotCombo.

'Whew, that was close,' whispered Refresh.

He couldn't contact Icon as they'd agreed a Visi-Tel silence until Icon was back in the central control module, but he could contact Tooltip and Media and update them on the situation on the scrambler channel.

'Tooltip, Refresh here, come in.'

'Tooltip, Tooltip! Refresh here, come in,' he repeated with more emphasis.

'Tooltip here, Refresh. Tooltip switch to scrambler channel 277 and confirm.'

Tooltip replies, 'On scrambler now. Are you still fighting the Happy Virus?'

'No, DotCombo told us to stop and I'm on my way to the Millennium Game Disc. DotCombo thinks that Ram and the Bugs are messing up all the games.'

'Where's Media? Has she gone with you?' asked Refresh.

'No, DotCombo has sent her to the Fashions Through the Millennium Disk.'

'What for?' exclaimed Refresh.

'DotCombo says that Ram and the Bugs are planning to steal all the clothes. Media left about 10 web minutes ago.'

The more I hear, the more worrying these get, thought Refresh.

'Look Tooltip, there's something wrong here. Don't go to the Millennium Games Disk, finish off the Happy Virus left on the internet and then contact me before you do anything else.'

'But Refresh, DotCombo instructed me to go. I can't disobey her orders!'

'Listen Tooltip, something's going on here, which I haven't worked out yet and until I do, we need to stick to the original plan. I've sent Icon back to the central control module on a contact blackout until he's with DotCombo in person. DotCombo thinks he's still with me so if she contacts you, that's what you think too, okay. Please do as I ask, Tooltip. It's my decision, I'll take the responsibility if it all goes wrong,' said Refresh.

'What about Media?' asked Tooltip.

'I'll contact her on the scrambler channel. From here on, all communication with me on the Visi-Tels is via the scrambler channel. If the situation is as bad as I think then we need to keep this to ourselves, the fewer who know the better,' said Refresh.

'Got you, Refresh. I'm with you,' said Tooltip. 'I'll turn and go back to the area where the last of the Happy Virus are concentrated.'

Tooltip knew Refresh wouldn't take these decisions without a good reason.

'Media, where are you, over?' asked Refresh.

'I'm in the readme zone of the Fashions Through the Millennium Disk. I'm just about to enter the tracks,' said Media.

'Media, if you're not on the scramble channel then switch it on,' said Refresh.

'I'm already scrambled,' said Media. 'What's up?'

'There's something going on which I can't explain just now, mainly because I haven't worked it out yet. But I believe Ram's behind a plan to split up the Surf_Aces in all directions so that his real plans don't fail. I don't know how he's doing it, but I've received very conflicting messages from DotCombo and I've sent Icon back to the central control module on a voice blackout until he's with DotCombo in person,' he continued. 'Media, I want you to listen to me and do as I tell you,' said Refresh.

Media liked Refresh in this commanding mood. *My*

hero, she thought.

'I want you to head for the Animal Kingdom Disk and rendezvous with me in the main jungle area. By the time you get here, Icon should be with DotCombo and we'll get this cleared up,' said Refresh.

'What if you're wrong?' asked Media.

'Let's not think about that until we have Icon with DotCombo,' said Refresh. 'I've sent Tooltip back to deal with the Happy Virus problem, Cache and Scanner will be in the HistoryLand Disk by now, so that's covered. If you head for here then our original plan is still workable. If I'm wrong and there are problems in the Beach Baby and Fashions Through the Millennium Disks we'll have to deal with that when we have more information. We've no other choice right now but to stick to the new plan.'

'Okay, I'm on my way,' said Media. 'I'll surf as fast as I can.'

'Scanner, come in. Over,' said Refresh.

'Scanner here.'

'Scanner, I received a message from DotCombo saying that you told her the little e-mail who died laughing was not telling the truth about the attack in the Animal Kingdom Disk. Is this correct?' said Refresh.

'Not on your life, Refresh. I haven't spoken to DotCombo since I left to meet Cache,' said Scanner.

'What's going on then? I had a discussion with DotCombo telling Icon and me to leave the Animal Kingdom Disk as the planned attack was a hoax,' said

Refresh. 'Scanner, can you get intelligence on what Ram has been doing today. Use all your contacts and make sure your search engine and browser are working properly. This is serious Scanner, be quick,' said Refresh. 'Is Cache there?'

'Yes,' said Scanner.

'Tell him to switch his Visi-Tel to the scrambler channel 277 and I'll call him.'

Scanner and Cache were making good progress; they had about twenty web kilometres to go before they reached the Tyrannosaurus Rex feeding grounds.

'Cache, Refresh here, over.'

'Hey good buddy,' said Cache, lively as always. 'What's happening, Refresh? We're almost within sight of the Tyrannosaurus Rex.'

'Cache, something is wrong. I'm getting conflicting messages from DotCombo. The other Surf_Aces are being given new orders by her to go to Disks we haven't had any intelligence of Ram Router and the Bugs attacking.

'She also said that Scanner had information that the attack on the Animal Kingdom Disc was a hoax and that the little e-mail was lying. I'm worried, Cache. Ram is up to something, but I don't know what it is! I've sent Icon back to the central control module and told him not to speak to anyone until he's with DotCombo in person,' said Refresh.

'Sounds bad, pal,' said Cache. 'What're you planning?'

'I've asked Scanner to get me all the intelligence he

can on what Ram has been doing today and get back to me as quickly as possible,' said Refresh. 'You continue with the Tyrannosaurus Rex situation, I think this will happen so beware.

'I've asked Media to join me here and I've sent Tooltip to finish off all of the remaining Happy Virus, that way we stick to as much of the original plan as possible until we can reach DotCombo.'

'Sounds good to me, I'd do exactly the same,' said Cache.

This reassured Refresh, to have the great Cache Downloader give him his seal of approval was very welcome and spurred Refresh to stick to his feelings and hold the plan together. Refresh was now confident his intuition was correct. Ram was up to something – but what?

DotCombo sat at her control module, she could not be certain why she had a feeling of foreboding, and she just felt that all wasn't well. It wasn't like the Surf_Aces to be so quiet. Okay they knew their jobs and what they had to do, but never had she sat waiting for information like this before.

What's going on? she thought, sipping on her juice.

She considered calling Refresh again. After all, her earlier conversation with him had been strange. Icon would never have left his Visi-Tel behind; the Surf_Aces are on attack mode so to do this was irresponsible. Something was wrong.

'Scanner, Cache come in. Over,' said DotCombo. 'What's happening, are you on the site yet?'

'Cache here, DotCombo. We're about eleven web kilometres from the Tyrannosaurus Rex feeding grounds.'

'Let me know when you see action,' said DotCombo. 'Scanner, have you heard from the Surf_Aces, any of them?'

'Yes, Refresh called me about 5 web minutes ago,' said Scanner.

'What did he want?' asked DotCombo.

'He wanted to know if I could find out what Ram has been up to today.'

'Why? Did he say, his reasons?'

'Nnnnno, he didn't,' stammered Scanner.

'Scanner!' shouted DotCombo. 'I want to know what's going on. I'm in the dark here. What's wrong?'

DotCombo was very very angry.

'Don't know DotCombo, just acting on a request from a Surf_Ace,' replied Scanner.

'I'll ask him myself,' said DotCombo. 'Over and out. Refresh, DotCombo here, come in.'

'Refresh here, DotCombo.'

'What's going on Refresh? I've had no contact from the Surf_Aces since I sent you all out this morning and don't expect me to believe that Icon/Visi-Tel story you gave me earlier!' she barked.

Refresh knew that only the real DotCombo would speak to him like this. 'DotCombo there's a problem, I don't know what it is but I've put a blackout on all communications between the Surf_Aces and you until I work it out,' said Refresh. 'Messages have been coming from you telling the Surf_Aces to go to different Disks and saying that the attack on the Animal Kingdom is a hoax.'

'I haven't spoken to any Surf_Aces apart from our conversation about half a web hour ago,' replied DotCombo.

'That's what I thought, DotCombo. But how could I be sure it wasn't you?'

'I see what you mean, Refresh. Do you think someone has hacked into our system and is sending messages to confuse us?'

'No, I think that Ram has found a way of mimicking your voice,' said Refresh. 'When you told me about the hoax it was your voice, for sure, but it wasn't your style, your way with words or mannerisms,' said Refresh.

'I see,' said DotCombo. 'It's Ram isn't it?'

'Yes, I've sent Icon back to the central control module to speak to you in person. I had no choice. I have rescinded all the rogue messages you gave, well we think you gave to Tooltip and Media.'

'I haven't spoken to Tooltip nor Media at all since the Happy Virus escapade today!' exclaimed DotCombo.

'Tooltip is back fighting the remnants of the Happy Virus and Media is on her way to me, I think we'll see an attack here shortly,' said Refresh.

'Good work, Refresh,' said DotCombo. 'Get the information you need from Scanner and report back to me. Scanner, you had better be working hard. Refresh needs information urgently,' said DotCombo.

'I'm on it DotCombo, I'm on it,' said Scanner. 'I've got some details, give me a couple of web minutes and I'll be ready.'

Meanwhile Cache and Scanner had arrived at the Tyrannosaurus Rex feeding grounds.

'DotCombo, Cache here, over.'

'Hear you,' said DotCombo.

'We have arrived at the Tyrannosaurus Rex feeding grounds. Can you send me all the information you have about their environment, what they eat, how fast they run, other types of dinosaurs in the area, what animals they will try to catch and any ideas on their weaknesses. I want as much information as you have available.'

'Sending now, load it on your Visi-Tel and you'll get images too. Cache, be careful,' said DotCombo. 'Remember that the Tyrannosaurus Rex are fearsome and you'll have Bugs to deal with too.'

Cache waited and then keyed his access code into his Visi-Tel.

'Scanner, you had better back-up this information in case we get separated,' said Cache. 'Accessing, information now visible,' he said as the data downloaded.

'DotCombo, it looks quiet here with no sign of any Tyrannosaurus Rex. Scanner will take a look around and I'll wait here in the feeding grounds,' said Cache.

Cache soaked up the information DotCombo had sent. It made interesting reading. He hadn't had to deal with Tyrannosaurus Rex or anything like them in the past. Most of the problems on the original internet were technical. In the early days, the US military had handed the system database and operational know-how over to the large software houses to allow them to develop programmes for general use. The internet then became a giant communications network available to everyone with a personal computer. There were no real dangers like the kind experienced now, but this wasn't due to the internet or its capabilities, technical or otherwise. It was Ram Router and his Bugs who were the real threat now.

Of course, Cache understood Ram better than anyone. If Ram was indeed planning to release the Tyrannosaurus Rex onto the open plains Cache would have his work cut out, make no mistake. But Cache had a new weapon; a revolutionary new weapon and it would soon be in action as the Tyrannosaurus Rex attack began.

TYRANNOSAURUS REX AND THE LASER GLOVES

'Now, what have we here?' Cache muttered softly as he looked at his Visi-Tel. 'Tyrannosaurus, the "Tyrant Lizard". Mmmmm, a big bad guy by the looks of it,' Cache mused. 'Tell me more,' he commanded the Visi-Tel. The Visi-Tel switched to audio.

'A large bipedal flesh eater with a huge head, eyes forward facing and jaws big enough to swallow a human.'

'Ouch!' exclaimed Cache. 'Sounds sore!'

The Visi-Tel continued its audio.

The Tyrannosaurus Rex has a short muscular neck and is broad chested with narrow hips. The Tyrannosaurus Rex has teeth, some of which could be at least twelve centimetres long. It is three toed, but has tiny arms with two fingers on each hand. It is about five to thirteen metres in length and was found in North America and Asia during what was known as the Cretaceous period. On the open plains they could reach speeds of over thirty-five kilometres per hour. They liked to chase duckbilled dinosaurs by lunging forward and taking deep bites! In the forest areas they would hide and startle their prey by jumping out from behind trees where they would hide patiently.

'Like him already,' said Cache, switching off his Visi-Tel.

Cache knew if the Bugs were serious about releasing the Tyrannosaurus Rex his ability to deal with the situation would depend on his keen mind as much as his physical abilities.

'Weeble, weeble, weeble,' sounds came from just over the horizon.

'Here we go,' said Cache. 'Scanner, anything where you are?'

'Yes, just coming into my search engine are pictures of Bugs, millions of them!'

'Get back here,' said Cache. 'We won't know what they are really planning until they're almost on top of us, so I don't want them to find out we're here.'

'I'll be with you in about thirty web seconds,' said Scanner.

The Bugs entering the HistoryLand Disk were in high spirits. Ram had prepared them well. Since what was originally just a diversion would now be a full-scale battle meant that the Bugs liked it much better!

'Weeble, weeble, weeble. We're on the scene, Ram. No dinosaurs around at the moment, perhaps they're hiding!' said the Bugs.

When they spoke in unison it sounded unreal. Can you imagine it? Millions of Bugs all talking at the same time, noisy or what?

Ram was still sitting at his console. He flicked to 'OFF' the voice simulator switch and leaned forward. 'Bugs, now the others have just arrived in the HistoryLand Disk you can start the attack on the Animal Kingdom Disk so let's go make mayhem! Be on your way my little terrors and have fun!' He laughed, his large colourful frame rising and falling and his shoulders heaving. He looked like a rainbow in perpetual motion!

The Bugs moved about excitedly as they gathered themselves into the typical Bug horde and set off to the domain exit, weebling happily as they left.

'That's my Bugs,' said Ram proudly.

'Weeble, weeble, weeble, I'm the hip hop horrible Bug,' said 3H.

'Weeble, weeble, weeble, I've a rap for this,' he said.

I'm the hip hop horrible Bug, 3H is my name,
I'm a rapper who's smarter and for danger I'm
     game… yesssss,
The dinosaurs are waiting they really don't
know,

We go, oh yes we go,
To bash the Surf_Aces,
And steal the show,
What am I like, what can I do?
I'm the hip hop horrible Bug, know me, 3H, Ya
Boo!

'Scares the life out of me,' said Ram, shaking his head. 'Now on your bike,' he rasped. 'You go rap with the others and make it good.'

3H, the little brown Bug with the hat and glasses, shook a left leg, weeble, weeble, weeble, and scampered off smartly to catch up with the horde of Bugs now nearing the domain exit.

162

'Bugs in HistoryLand, give me progress report,' Ram shouted into his command pod. 'Are the Tyrannosaurus Rex out and running yet?'

'Weeble, weeble, weeble, we think there are some hiding in the forest. About 4.2 million of us are going in to take a look,' said the Bugs.

'Report in ten web minutes, I want action!' said Ram.

The forest was dark and a bit creepy. The Bugs entered slowly.

'Weeble, weeble, weeble, shooosh, shooosh, try to keep it quite,' called 3H.

Scanner returned as Cache readied himself for action.

'This new DBM any good?' he said to Scanner.

'It worked for Tooltip, it splattered the Happy Virus all over the place,' replied Scanner.

'Tyrannosaurus Rex are something else and there will be millions of Bugs,' said Cache worriedly.

'Don't worry Cache. It'll work. The Surf_Aces use them all the time and they've never failed yet. Try the new sound lock on device, then you don't need to actually point at your target.'

'Listen Scanner, I want to attack the Bugs the minute we catch sight of them. I don't want to have to fight Bugs and the Tyrannosaurus Rex at the same time.'

'Cache, I agree. But if the Bugs release the Tyrannosaurus Rex we'll need to stop them reaching the open plains first, even if it means letting the Bugs escape,' said Scanner.

'Bugs don't get to escape from Cache Downloader!'

'Cache, don't let your old scores get in the way. We've a job to do here.'

'I know, I know,' said Cache. 'It's difficult to ignore them, especially when I see the Bugs. It reminds me of that rascal Ram Router and what he did to me.'

'Work first,' said Scanner. 'Focus your mind, we can sort out Ram another time,' he continued, trying to keep Cache concentrated on the imminent problem.

'Weeble, weeble, weeble, Tyrannosaurus Rex over there!' shouted the Bugs.

'Weeble, weeble, weeble, attack plan into operation, weeble, weeble, weeble here we go.'

There were about seven Tyrannosaurus Rex wandering in the forest area.

'Weeble, weeble, weeble. Tyrannosaurus Rex here we come.'

The Bugs moulded together to form a giant probe. Running at pace, they battered the protection fences down bursting into the area with the force of a Surf_Ace at eight quantum calamities!

'Weeble, weeble, weeble!' they shouted as they chased after the Tyrannosaurus Rex. The startled dinosaurs headed for the probe anticipating a meal!

'Weeble, weeble, weeble, faster, faster!' the Bugs shouted. 'Weeble, weeble, weeble, yeehaaa, keep moving!'

'Scanner, look!' said Cache pointing towards the forest area. 'Let's go. DotCombo, over,' said Cache, forgetting to switch to the scrambler channel on his Visi-Tel. 'Attack started, the Bugs are trying to herd a group of Tyrannosaurus Rex towards a gap they've made in the protection fences.'

Ram picked up the message.

'That sounds like Cache Downloader, what's he doing in there?'

Switching on the voice simulator, Ram cleared his throat and spoke, 'Cache, this is DotCombo, over,' said Ram. 'The Bugs are too strong and there's too many of them for you, leave immediately.'

'What?' said Cache. 'No way, the attack's started!' replied Cache in amazement.

Then he remembered his conversation with Refresh, it was Ram and not DotCombo who he was speaking to.

Cache realised his error and said, 'DotCombo, you're right. Okay we'll withdraw to a safe position and report our status, over.'

Ram chuckled, 'That dope Downloader thinks he'll outsmart Ram Router does he?'

Ram switched the voice simulator to 'OFF' and waited.

Cache was annoyed at his error. 'Stupid, eh Scanner? Let's say we go get us some Bugs.'

Scanner nodded in approval.

'Right, let's go,' said Cache.

The Bugs were now in complete control, their probe was pushing the Tyrannosaurus Rex out of the forest area and towards the open plains.

'Scanner, I'm going to head towards the group of Bugs and see if I can pick off some as a warning. It might just stop them in their tracks.'

'I'll browse from here and keep you up to date on the wider picture,' said Scanner.

'Scanner, you be my eyes and ears. I'll need intelligence and back-up if things get sticky, so be ready to pitch in and help.'

Cache didn't have the advantage of the Surf_Aces latest magnetic boards; his version was a little older to say the least! What he lacked in speed he made up for in agility. Cache in his prime was the equal of any of the current Surf_Aces, at least that's what he thought! He fired some warning shots from the DBM and laser flashes picked off some Bugs who 'Weeble, weeble, weeble'd,' as they leapt into the air screaming and exploding.

'Reset DBM to sound lock on device, Cache,' said Scanner. 'It'll help and you can fire at random.'

Cache glided purposefully, skimming the surface of the forest floor as he weaved in and out of the trees and bushes. He straightened and with his DBM held out in front of him, he fired rapidly in the direction of the Bugs who were still probe shaped. Laser beams shot out all over the place, Bugs screamed and exploded. Cache moved his body from side to side to avoid making himself a target, and then he fired at the centre of the probe shape. A huge and loud bang erupted as thousands of Bugs were thrown into the air, screaming and exploding like colourful firecrackers!

The sound sprattled and frazzled, popping sounds filled the air, but still the probe advanced. Cache fired again and much the same thing happened, lots of screaming and sprattling but not much stopping.

'Weeble, weeble, weeble can't stop us, can't stop us!' the Bugs shouted.

You watch this, thought Cache.

'Scanner, get down here fast!' he shouted into his Visi-Tel. Scanner was off like a shot. He arrived in a blur at Cache's side where he screeched to a halt.

'Scanner, I want you to head for the probe. Be careful to avoid the Tyrannosaurus Rex as you skirt around them,' said Cache.

'What's the plan?' said Scanner excitedly. He liked being involved in the action.

'I want you to get around the probe and scan it in all directions into your memory bank.'

'Then what?' asked Scanner.

'Once we've a picture of the shape I want you to switch your visor over to closed. I'm going to sound lock on and send multiple laser beams from the DBM in all directions,' said Cache. 'Now the tricky bit,' he continued. 'We transfer the picture to my Visi-Tel, I'll adjust the DBM sound lock on to match the picture. As I fire the DBM, I need you to hover at speed all over the place.'

'You mean you're going to fire at me,' said Scanner, getting the picture.

'No Scanner, I'm going to feed the picture and sound lock on into the DBM and then fire at the picture in the memory, like a remote game console, I'll be firing using the picture. What I want you to do is to move around as fast as you can so that the laser beams bounce off your visor and back towards the Bugs. That way we'll get maximum effect and damage.'

'You're firing at me!' exclaimed Scanner.

'I'm not,' said Cache. 'I'm firing at the picture, you're, if you like, getting in the way of the beams as they dart about and deflect them around the probe. This way we'll kill more Bugs and it might just weaken them enough to go in hard and finish them off properly,' said Cache with complete confidence.

'How do I know one of the beams won't miss my visor?' said a very worried Scanner.

'That's where you need to move around fast, making sure each beam you get in front of hits your visor and only your visor! You can do it Scanner, remember I programmed you so I know this'll work.'

'When you put it like that Cache, it's very reassuring, but I'm still scared.'

'Scanner, Scanner, trust me,' said Cache. 'Come on, no time to lose,' said Cache, his voice hardening.

Scanner headed for the probe as Cache continued to fire randomly at the front and sides. Bugs flew into the air screaming and exploding.

As Scanner weaved around he was aware that the situation was becoming increasingly difficult, he could see Cache surfing about.

He seemed to be everywhere as he fired his DBM into the probe.

Scanner did his job well and quickly, managing to avoid not only the Bugs but also the Tyrannosaurus Rex as he glided about up and over, over and under the probe, capturing every minuscule portion.

'Ready Cache!' he called into his control.

'Right, let me have the picture,' said Cache.

'Downloading to Downloader!' said Scanner, laughingly.

'Joking?' said Cache. 'Wait until I start firing!'

Scanner winced and sighed deeply.

Cache started to fire, using the picture as his map.

'Scanner move, move!' shouted Cache into his Visi-Tel.

Scanner shot about at speeds he never knew he had as laser beams bounced around.

Scanner knew he'd have to get in the way of as many as he could.

'Doing good,' shouted Cache.

Bugs were blasted in all directions as a hail of laser beams washed over them from all angles.

'Weeble, weeble, weeble!' screamed the Bugs as they exploded.

Suddenly the Tyrannosaurus Rex turned back towards the probe that was now more a pile of misshapen Bugs. As if realising the danger, the remaining Bugs moulded into a tank, a giant modern weapon of mass destruction. This was not what Cache wanted, the Tyrannosaurus Rex heading back towards the Bugs and the Bugs turning into something different. This wasn't the picture he now had in his

Visi-Tel. The tank fired and the Tyrannosaurus Rex dispersed as they fled in all directions. Chaos!

'Scanner, trouble. Open your visor and scan the new shapes,' said Cache.

'The tank's firing shots into the air!' said Scanner. 'I don't think I can get a clear picture, but I'll try,' he said as he burst off back towards the tank.

The Tyrannosaurus Rex were now running at speed towards the open plains and were being pursued by the tank which was firing at them.

'This is bad, Scanner,' said Cache into his Visi-Tel. 'Look, get me the best picture you can and we'll try again.'

'I'll try my best,' said Scanner working his way through the bursts of fire.

Scanner, unless he moved quickly, was now a real target. This was worse than the laser beams.

'Careful Scanner,' said Cache.

'Got it!' cried Scanner.

'Great, download,' said Cache.

'It's there, it's all there!' said Scanner.

'Right, here we go again, same routine as before.'

Laser beams and tank fires were everywhere. It was now a battle zone as the Bugs chased the Tyrannosaurus Rex out of the forest and towards the open plains.

'Weeble, weeble, weeble, thanks for the help!' they called to Cache and Scanner.

'Weeble, weeble, weeble. Ram, Tyrannosaurus Rex heading for the open plains!' called the Bugs.

'Ram here, nice work Bugs. Any sign of Mr Downloader and his trusty Scanner?'

'Weeble, weeble, weeble, he's here, but struggling. We're now a tank, the probe didn't work so we converted.'

Cache steadied himself and he again fired at random. Laser beams shot across the tank and Scanner darted in front of as many as he could.

'Blast!' said Cache. 'This isn't working fast enough.'

'Scanner, get back here again, we've more talking to do.'

'On my way,' said Scanner. He was relieved!

The tank complete with the seven Tyrannosaurus Rex was well out of the forest now and the open plains beckoned. The open plains are a beautiful sight and covered in masses of small animals.

'Scanner, the DBMs are good and we could stop the Bugs and their tank, but there's not enough firepower to deal with the amount of Bugs here, never mind the Tyrannosaurus Rex.'

'What can we do?' asked Scanner, whirring about and scanning the scene around him.

'Laser gloves!' said Cache. 'I've been looking for a good reason to try them out.'

'The laser what?' exclaimed Scanner.

'New invention, been waiting to test it in a real situation for a long time,' said Cache reaching into his backpack.

It looked like a wire mesh oven glove; it was thick and a silvery colour.

'We'll get some action in now,' said Cache.

'What does it do?' Scanner asked, puzzled, scratching his head scanner with his voice probe.

'Well Scanner my old robotic buddy, this is the future. The DBM will become extinct,' Cache said. 'The Surf_Aces will go crazy for this one when they see it! I've made two, one for each hand. They're programmed and ready to go. I've just never found a use for them until now.

'Attached to a laser unit here on my waist belt, it fires beams from the fingers. All you have to do is point and the Bugs are well and truly blasted. Weeble, they'll weeble no more!' Cache laughed.

'What a weapon,' said Scanner. 'Is it powerful, I mean, really powerful?'

'I'll show you power,' said Cache, putting on one glove and pointing in the direction of a large boulder.

With a twist of his wrist, laser beams shot from each finger.

There was an enormous explosion. When the smoke cleared the boulder didn't exist except for a pile of dust where the boulder had been a few web seconds ago.

'Wow!' said Scanner. 'How did you dream that one up?'

'You know I like to play the laser harp?'

'Sure,' said Scanner, 'but I don't understand the whole laser harp thing.'

'The laser harp is an instrument similar to a harp, hence its name,' said Cache. 'On a conventional harp there are strings of different lengths going from top to bottom, the laser harp simply has laser beams instead. The laser beams are set at different lengths too. You see Scanner, on a conventional harp the strings are plucked to make sounds. The laser harp works to the same principle. Except instead of plucking, if a particular beam is broken by putting an object in between it will sound a note.

'By pushing an object through the beams a tune can be played. But, and the big but is that only a very special object can be used and it has to be made from a specific material. Without special protection the laser beam will burn a hole straight through the skin!' continued Cache.

'I've found a special compound material, like a kind of mesh, and I made it into the shape of a glove that allows me to play by punching through each laser beam. One day I was experimenting and I thought if I could make the DBM smaller, it could fit into each finger of the glove. Since the glove is laser proof there would be no danger to the person firing. I took an old DBM and dismantled it, worked on it and finally had a prototype I could use,' said Cache. 'Inside each finger there is a tiny miniature DBM, but this one packs a bigger kick! What you see here is the finished article,' said Cache. 'One on each hand, point, a twist of the wrist and flash, bang and Bugs are zapped! You can point and operate one finger or as many as you like!' exclaimed Cache.

'The Surf_Aces will love this!' said Scanner.

'I hope to convince DotCombo to give me the funds to make more,' said Cache. 'But we need to be careful, the material compound is a secret and I don't want it to fall into the wrong hands, if you get my drift.'

'You mean like Ram Router and the Bugs,' said Scanner.

'Got it in one,' said Cache. 'Can you imagine millions of Bugs wearing laser gloves? The thought scares me to death!' said Cache.

'What a dreadful thought, but while you have the only version, and I presume no one has seen it yet, what's the problem?' questioned Scanner.

'Think about it, Scanner. I gave you a brain, so use it. Why shouldn't we be found out?'

'You're about to use it!' exclaimed Scanner. 'You're about to use it, that's it!' he shouted excitedly.

'Right, once we use it not only will the Bugs see it, but it will also be relayed back to Ram on the Bugs antennae,' said Cache.

'He wasn't called Ram Router for nothing!' said Scanner. 'He misses nothing, that's for sure!'

'Now the secret's out of the bag, or backpack in this case,' smiled Cache, 'and if it's as successful as I think, Ram will have to get his hands on the technology. Once we deal with this problem we'll soon have another, so let's get to work,' said Cache.

'The Bugs have almost all the Tyrannosaurus Rex on the open plains, their tank is herding them about like cattle,' said Scanner, moving his head scans about and absorbing all the data he could.

'I want that tank out of business,' interjected Cache. 'I want you to do the same as before, Scanner,' he said. 'Get round behind the Tyrannosaurus Rex and get me as much visible information as possible, I want my Visi-Tel full of data. The laser glove will fire rapidly, ten beams at a time, and I want to aim directly at the centre of the Bugs' tank. That way we'll blow a hole in their scheme! Go Scanner and stay on vision and voice at all times,' instructed Cache, pulling on his other laser glove.

Scanner sped off. At his best he could get to four maybe five quantum calamities and if he tried really hard he could reach around ten web metres above the ground. Scanner's magnetic field needed upgrading and he hoped that DotCombo would get around to it soon so that he could travel as fast and as high as the Surf_Aces. His head scan looked around and below as he soared past. Scanner liked the open plains in the HistoryLand Disk.

It really was beautiful, this was how the earth looked millions of years ago, fresh, clean and beautiful.

He saw the huge trees and bushes in the distance, where the forest canopy started again. The open plains were really a large area of forest that had been destroyed by fire hundreds of thousands of years ago. Instead of trees and bushes they now boasted vast grassland, in the middle of which sat a massive waterhole used by all the little animals.

'Nearly there!' Scanner called into his relay system.

'Got you,' said Cache, now armed with both laser gloves.

He had to be careful not to make any jerky movements with his wrists or any of his fingers could fire off a laser beam.

Wouldn't want to shoot myself in the foot, he thought to himself.

His magnetic board quivered at his side as Cache stepped on and immediately surfed off towards the open plains. On his Visi-Tel he could see pictures of the Bugs' tank and the Tyrannosaurus Rex out in front.

'Need an update,' Ram called from his console.

'Weeble, weeble, weeble!' called the Bugs. 'Weeble, weeble, weeble, we're a TANK, we're a TANK!'

'I can see that and you told me earlier. Probe didn't work, probe didn't work eh?' Ram spat into his microphone.

'Weeble, weeble, weeble, Cache Downloader was picking us off at random.'

'Well you had better get on with it, we're about to start the attack on the Animal Kingdom Disk so you guys out there need to keep Cache busy,' said Ram.

'Weeble, weeble, weeble, we're having fun, we're having fun,' called the Bugs.

Ram could see Cache and Scanner on his vision system. In fact, he could see the whole drama unfolding.

Ram muttered as he watched, 'Cache Downloader, look at him surfing about like some superstar athlete, he'll need to go and soon.' He glared into his console, then shouted, 'Bugs!'

'Weeble, weeble, weeble,' and about 27.2 million Bugs appeared.

'Animal Kingdom Disk attack team, I want the rare tiger captured and brought back here,' said Ram. 'Now listen carefully, you multicoloured terrors. There'd better be no mistakes and no screw ups,' barked Ram.

'Weeble, weeble, weeble,' and out from the crowd stepped a little purple Bug who shook its left leg and said, 'Weeble, weeble, weeble, I have a poem.'

'Rapping, wind machines and now poems,' said Ram. 'Next we'll have a group or an orchestra. You lot are here to cause trouble and what do I get? Rapping, poems and music!'

'Weeble, weeble, weeble, it's a belter!' said the little purple Bug.

'If you must,' said Ram.

'Weeble, weeble, weeble,' suddenly the little purple Bug sneezed and flew backwards, embedding himself by the antennae in a lump of Gloob!

'Is this part of the poem?' said Ram. 'If it is it's a pretty impressive intro!' he laughed loudly.

Several Bugs scampered over to where the little purple Bug twanged up and down and from side to side, they started to pull it by the feet.

Stretching and heaving they pulled as hard as they could, when suddenly there was a splatting sound as the little purple Bug was pulled free and took the Bugs rescuing it off at speed across the domain. They ended huddled in a writhing mass some twenty web metres from where Ram sat watching, shaking his head in dismay.

'If I wanted a floor show I would have ordered one!' he bellowed.

'Weeble, weeble, weeble, sorry about that,' said the little purple Bug, dusting himself down. 'Weeble, weeble, weeble, I'll start my poem now.'

'Go on, but it'll have to be good to follow that last act!' Ram laughed.

The Bugs cheered him. Their antics kept the domain alight with humour despite the nasty nature of those who inhabited the place.

Weeble, weeble, weeble,
Who is our leader it has to be Ram,
A colourful guy, a right Mr Nasty, so good in a
    jam,
With his bright multicoloured garment,
He's got to be the number one fashion
    statement,
What's his message the Bugs all ask,
It's an end to the Surf_Aces that's our task!
Weeble, weeble, weeble that's my poem, like it
    Ram?

'One of the best, what do you think?' Ram shouted to the assembled hordes.

'Weeble, weeble, weeble,' shouts rose from the millions of Bugs.

The little purple Bug shook a left leg and

disappeared back into the crowd.

'Now hear me,' said Ram. 'I don't want this attack to fail, it's too important and I want that tiger. The attack in the HistoryLand Disk seems to be going well after a little setback,' said Ram. 'So we need to get going if we're to keep those Surf_Aces busy. Off you go, Bugs, and keep me informed of progress.'

Flicking the 'ON' switch Ram coughed and spoke into the DotCombo voice simulator.

'Oh Surf_Aces, where are you?'

Nothing. Not a sound.

'Blast! I hope this still works, where's that little Bug Yellow?'

'Weeble, weeble, weeble he's gone off with the others,' said a really little chequered Bug, puffing and panting.

'What happened to you?' said Ram.

'Weeble, weeble, weeble, my antennae ball fell off and I had to come back for it.'

'Get after the Bugs and order the little Yellow Bug to come back here quickly,' said Ram. 'Tell him the voice doesn't simulate!'

'Weeble, weeble, weeble, okay, I will,' said the really little chequered Bug, still drawing breath.

'I'll try it again,' said Ram to himself.

He flicked the 'OFF' and 'ON' switch several times, 'Modern technology,' he muttered. 'Hate it, never works when you want it to!'

He flicked 'ON' and spoke into the simulator, 'Oh Surf_Aces, where are you? It's DotCombo here.'

Still nothing!

'Blast!' said Ram, not realising that the Surf_Aces were running a silence scam on Refresh's instructions. Ram thought the voice simulator wasn't working!

Icon had just arrived back at the central control module where DotCombo sat patiently.

'I don't like these voice blackouts,' she said as Icon entered the module. 'Icon, good to see you,' said DotCombo.

Icon glided across to where DotCombo sat, he always had to have a little shimmy and a wiggle from side to side on his magnetic board, and it was a kind of visual signature. From a distance you always knew it was Icon by his unique surfing style.

'DotCombo, Refresh thinks Ram's up to something. We've been getting messages from you that don't make sense,' said Icon.

'Refresh wants to go live as soon as I have returned, if I'm with you then we can confirm that it's really you who's giving the orders. I'm going to call Refresh now on the scrambler channel, then we'll switch to normal,' said Icon.

'Refresh, come in,' said Icon.

'Refresh here, switch to normal.'

DotCombo watched silently, she knew that if the problem was real the Surf_Aces had to fix it.

'Hi Icon,' said Refresh. 'Ready to return?'

'Yes,' said Icon.

Ram had picked up the conversation, which was exactly what the Surf_Aces wanted.

He fiddled with the 'OFF' and 'ON' switch again and said, 'Oh Surf_Aces where are you? It's DotCombo here,' said Ram.

DotCombo immediately straightened up in her seat.

'That's Ram Router!' she exclaimed. 'The rascal's impersonating my voice! Let him keep talking, I want to hear more,' she said.

'Oh Refresh, come in,' said Ram.

'Refresh here, DotCombo.'

'Have you left the Animal Kingdom Disk yet?'

'Yes, I'm heading back to the central control module,' said Refresh.

That's a good Surf_Ace, thought Ram smirking to himself.

'Where's Icon? Is he still with you?' asked Ram.

'Yes he is,' said Refresh.

'Good,' said Ram. 'I have sent Tooltip to the Millennium Games Disk and Media is in the Fashions Through the Millennium Disk, there are Bugs causing terrible problems there,' said Ram.

'Oh, that scoundrel!' said DotCombo.

'We'll be back in the central control module soon,' said Refresh.

'Good,' said Ram.

'No wait, there's apparently a problem developing. A bunch of Bugs have entered the Greatest Mysteries of Our Times Disk and are unravelling the mysteries. You and Icon head for there,' said Ram.

'Don't you dare,' said DotCombo quietly. Icon

looked at her and laughed.

'Okay,' said Refresh. 'I'm on my way.'

'Over and out Surf_Aces,' said Ram as he flicked the switch to 'OFF'.

That'll keep those two out of the way for a while, thought Ram.

Of course, Refresh had no intention of acting on this instruction, but he knew Ram had to believe that he was.

'Switch back to scramble channel all Surf_Aces,' said Refresh.

'What's happening?' asked Tooltip. 'I'm still fighting the Happy Virus and I'm nearly done, there's only one left over on the G66700435 routing junction,' he continued.

Refresh explained to Tooltip recent events.

'DotCombo,' said Refresh.

'DotCombo here. Well done Refresh, I think you've got Ram fooled.'

'I think so, DotCombo. But it won't be long before he finds out because we'll be visible as soon as the attack starts in the Animal Kingdom Disk.'

'I know, Refresh,' said DotCombo. 'But then he'll also know that the Surf_Aces are not obeying the instructions of DotCombo and he'll be puzzled and won't know why.'

'Listen DotCombo, Media is now here with me and we're waiting for an attack of some kind to start,' said Refresh. 'I think once Tooltip is finished with that last Happy Virus you should send him here to help us and send Icon to work with Cache Downloader and Scanner.'

'Sounds good to me,' said DotCombo. 'Surf_Aces, listen up!' commanded DotCombo. 'We have a major set of problems on the internet and various Disks. Refresh, Media and eventually Tooltip will work on the Animal Kingdom situation, Icon will immediately leave the central control module and work with Cache,' she paused. 'If anything else happens we'll deal with it as it occurs, for the moment I want all the Surf_Aces working in teams in the two known problem areas,' she continued.

Tooltip rounded the corner and took him from routing junction D5903992 towards where the Happy Virus sounds were coming from at routing junction G66700435.

'Ha, ha, ha, he, he, ho, ho,' sounds could be heard and were getting closer.

Suddenly Tooltip could see the Happy Virus. It was lying in wait for an e-mail that had taken the wrong route to its address but now appeared to be back on track. Tooltip glided carefully towards the scene, making sure not to alert the Happy Virus to his presence. He could see the e-mail now, but didn't want to have the same thing happen to him as before when he had dived in between the Happy Virus and the e-mail and ended up being wrapped in laughter! The e-mail looked left and right as it entered the routing junction. Tooltip planned to attack the Happy Virus before it saw the e-mail. He took a couple of surfing moves backwards sizing up the situation, when suddenly the e-mail stopped at the junction.

What's it doing, thought Tooltip as he hovered.

The Happy Virus waited silently. Tooltip could see both from his vantage point. The e-mail seemed to be waiting. But for what? Then Tooltip realised the e-mail was waiting for the next routing junction to lock onto it. There must be a delay in the next junction and it's not sent a signal. The e-mail waited.

'That's all I need!' said Tooltip as he primed his DBM.

The Happy Virus waited. Tooltip waited.

I'm going to attack, he thought, there's no sense in holding on.

The only problem was that, the now stationary e-mail made an easier target for the Happy Virus. If Tooltip attacked, the Happy Virus would be able to get to the e-mail easily. Since it wasn't moving it was a sitting target.

What to do, what to do? he thought.

I've got no choice I have to go in between the two of them again.

I'm going in at speed, he planned.

There'll be no messing with Tooltip this time.

The e-mail sat waiting. The Happy Virus sat waiting. Tooltip was on the move, waiting no longer. DBM fixed to sound lock on. He surfed off at high speed.

He could see the Happy Virus; it was still sitting quietly and waiting for the e-mail.

184

Tooltip thought, *if I surf past and at the same time do an overhead flip, the Happy Virus won't be able to react fast enough and I'll have it with one strike of my DBM.*

Tooltip was surfing fast now as he headed for the Happy Virus.

'No!' he shouted as the e-mail turned to look in his direction.

The Happy Virus heard Tooltip and immediately rounded on the e-mail. Tooltip was moving fast now and he flipped from side to side as he glided to where the e-mail sat.

'Get out of here,' shouted Tooltip at the e-mail.

He couldn't have known, but this e-mail was a wandering nitwit@dopey.com, an e-mail sent by pranksters and hackers to annoy the receiver. If this e-mail entered an end-user's address it wandered about unable to open, unable to do or say anything. In fact, it was a pest and worst of all it couldn't be erased once received.

Tooltip closed in on the Happy Virus, which had broken its cover, and was now laughing and laughing as it headed for the e-mail. Tooltip activated his sound lock on.

Ready as I'll ever be, he thought.

He fired rapidly, laser beams shot out in a mass of vibrant light.

The e-mail, being a nitwit@dopey.com, remained unfazed by the activity around it. Tooltip shot straight for the Happy Virus and hit it, but not clean enough to stop it. The Happy Virus was about three web metres from the e-mail. Suddenly the e-mail saw the Happy Virus and the shock and horror on its face was a treat. The e-mail tried to move but his routing signal hadn't arrived and he was completely immobile. In fact, the e-mail's routing signal had arrived but it just didn't have the brainpower to realise it. Tooltip was firing at the Happy Virus and shots burst off it together with loud screams. If he could get one clean hit it would all be over.

The e-mail still sat waiting and watching the Happy Virus getting closer and closer.

'DotCombo, come in. Over,' said Tooltip. 'Can you see this, the Happy Virus is closing in, I'm firing at it but the e-mail isn't moving. It's sitting and watching,' he continued. 'Strangest thing I've ever seen, any thoughts or ideas on how I can get it moving?'

'DotCombo, here. Over. Looks like you've got a nitwit@dopey.com on your hands.'

'I think I can finish off the Happy Virus, but if the e-mail stays put I don't think I can save it. The Happy Virus is too close and its power is bound to be felt by the e-mail.'

'Tooltip, it's a nitwit@dopey.com e-mail, take it out too!' said DotCombo.

'What? How do you know?' said Tooltip, still firing at the Happy Virus.

'The content will be rubbish, Tooltip. It always is,' said DotCombo. 'Take out the Happy Virus and the e-mail too and do it now!' said DotCombo.

'Will do,' said Tooltip.

He now had a different view on how to deal with the problem.

'I'll let the Happy Virus get right on top of the e-mail then I'll blow them both to smithereens,' he whispered to himself.

The Happy Virus was very close to the e-mail who stayed completely still, fear written all over its face! It seemed routed to the spot, signal or no signal this e-mail was stupid! The Happy Virus jumped and wrapped itself around the e-mail laughing and laughing. Tooltip drew back and watched, he'd weakened the Happy Virus so it could take a long time for the e-mail to die laughing. The e-mail started to jump up and down, shaking and laughing in a high-pitched voice.

'He, he, he, he, ho, ho, ho, he, ha, he, ha, ha!' it cried.

Tooltip could wait no longer, better to act now. He surfed towards the Happy Virus, which was now well and truly wrapped around the e-mail.

He primed his DBM again and swooped towards them, changing the setting on his DBM to maximum.

Blast, blast, blast and laser beams shot towards the Happy Virus. Bang! A massive explosion, the Happy Virus wrapped around the nitwit@dopey.com e-mail, soared into the air, burst into flames and dropped like sparkling dust particles towards the internet floor where they landed with a thump.

The Happy Virus wriggled in agony, the e-mail was gone.

The Happy Virus let out muted, abrupt laughing sounds, 'Hhhha, hhhho, hhooo, hhha, hhaaa, hhee, hoo, hhhhaaaaaa.' Then it slumped backwards and collapsed in a heap.

'Whew!' said Tooltip.

'DotCombo, all of the Happy Virus is finished.'

'Well done Tooltip, good work. Now head for the Animal Kingdom Disk. Refresh and Media will need your help,' replied DotCombo.

'On my way.'

Tooltip took one last look around; just to be sure he hadn't missed any of the Happy Virus. It was quiet, not a sound of laughter, well, not Happy Virus laughter anyway! He flipped Icon style and fell off his magnetic board!

'Must practice that more!' he laughed.

'Watch out Cache!' shouted Scanner. 'The tank is heading for you!'

'Got it in my sights,' said Cache.

The Bugs shaped as a tank were herding the Tyrannosaurus Rex right into the middle of the open plains as close to the watering hole as possible. This way the Tyrannosaurus Rex would have a better chance to eat as many of the little animals as possible.

Cache was coming at speed now. With his laser gloves ready he fired shot after shot. Laser beams blasted from his fingers. He'd quickly mastered the art of surfing, gliding and hovering, whilst at the same time firing with both arms outstretched. He could wave his arms about and still fire; it was a marvellous sight. As Cache struck the tank, Scanner would intercept any laser beams that overshot and send them back towards the tank. Bugs leapt screaming and exploding in all directions, a large hole was now visible in the tank.

One more go should do it, thought Cache.

'Scanner, we're going in one more time,' Cache said.

'Ready,' said Scanner.

Cache hovered from side to side, making mental pictures of the scene. A deep breath and he was off! His laser gloves were outstanding, beams shot at all angles and in all directions. The Bugs couldn't cope and quickly realised they needed to do something. The tank looked nothing like a tank any more. Well, it did but it resembled a tank with serious problems and injuries! Bugs flew everywhere screaming and exploding. Cache was now picking them off at will.

'Scanner?' said Cache.

'Yes?' Scanner replied.

'Scanner, get towards the Tyrannosaurus Rex and see if you can hold them where they are until I finish off the Bugs.'

'Okay Cache,' replied Scanner. 'I'm on my way.'

Cache took one more look at the dishevelled tank. He fired full blast at it and a brilliant explosion happened, Bugs flew everywhere.

'That's my boys!' shouted Cache. 'Exploding Bugs, great!'

A large heap of smouldering Bugs lay in various

stages of extinction. Bugs staggered about shaking their left legs and collapsing, some exploded like popcorn, some fizzled and others merely burst and dropped where they stood! Of the millions of Bugs who had entered the HistoryLand Disk, Cache reckoned about a hundred thousand remained. Although they looked a well-beaten bunch, it paid never to underestimate the Bugs.

Scanner had reached the Tyrannosaurus Rex now and was making movements and noises to attract their attention.

'Yoo hoo, Tyrannosaurus Rex!' he shouted, gliding and surfing around them.

'Careful Scanner!' shouted Cache having just arrived. 'We'll need to find a way to get them back.'

But the Tyrannosaurus Rex weren't interested in going back, they'd all the food they needed right here on the open plains. Little animals ran for their lives as the Tyrannosaurus Rex started to chase them, large jaws at the ready, claws bared with saliva dripping from their mouths. It was party time as far as the Tyrannosaurus Rex were concerned and they made giant strides towards the little animals. Several were already eating small antelopes and warthogs. Anything and everything that moved was their prey. A ferocious fight broke out between two Tyrannosaurus Rex over an ancient prehistoric wildebeest, the carcass being torn in two as the huge jaws ripped at the meat.

'Wow!' said Scanner. 'They just ripped it apart like tearing paper.'

'Listen Scanner,' said Cache, 'we need to do something to get these fellas back on the move and out of here.'

'Fire your laser gloves at their rear ends!' shouted Scanner.

'Weeble, weeble, weeble.'

'Where'd that come from?' said Cache, as he and Scanner turned to look.

Over the hill came what looked like another giant Tyrannosaurus Rex, but this one was different. The remaining Bugs had moulded into a Tyrannosaurus Rex and it was heading towards Cache and Scanner!

'They never give up, do they?' said Cache. 'Look at them now!'

'That's all we need,' said Scanner. 'One Tyrannosaurus Rex too many.'

'Right,' said Cache. 'Same plan as before, we'll herd the real Tyrannosaurus Rex back to the forest and we'll take out this fake one in the same way we did with the tank.'

The Bugs were snapping and snarling; this was a mean Tyrannosaurus Rex as it plodded over the hillside towards the open plains. Cache surfed towards it, firing his laser gloves. A beam crashed off its head sending another batch of Bugs screaming and exploding into the air.

'Good shot!' shouted Scanner.

'Get round behind the real Tyrannosaurus Rex,' said Cache.

'Come on Bugs, let's be having you!' shouted Cache.

His ability to move around at speed firing with both hands outstretched was unbelievable and his rapid fire had the Bugs troubled once more.

'Not working out today, Bugs!' he shouted.

'Weeble, weeble, weeble, we'll get you, Cache!' shouted the Bug shaped Tyrannosaurus Rex.

'Not if I get you first!' laughed Cache as he let off another round of laser beams.

Screams and explosions once more filled the air. Every now and then Cache would fire at the real Tyrannosaurus Rex to get them moving.

'Aaarrgghh, aaarrgghhh!' they cried, hurting from the laser blasts.

It wasn't working though because they still charged around picking off little animals as often as they liked. The skin of the Tyrannosaurus Rex was extremely thick and hard. Laser beams made an impression but from a distance the effect wasn't that great. Cache knew he'd need to get closer.

'Cache!' called Scanner.

'What?' replied Cache.

'Let me finish off the Bugs with the normal DBM and you round up the Tyrannosaurus Rex,' suggested Scanner. 'You could fix it to my voice pod and I'll activate it with my arm,' he continued.

'Good idea,' replied Cache. 'The Bugs are almost finished and you could tidy them up while I concentrate on those big fellas.'

'See, I've got good ideas too!' laughed Scanner.

'Just you be careful, Scanner. The Bugs aren't

finished yet, so watch yourself.'

Cache surfed off again towards the real Tyrannosaurus Rex. Crunch! Crack! The large jaws of a male Tyrannosaurus Rex bit into a little prehistoric antelope. Swish! Slap! The tail of another Tyrannosaurus Rex lashed out at an unsuspecting gazelle, a variety of which is now extinct and no wonder with these big killers about! Animals ran around in a blind panic, scattered in their thousands by the rampaging Tyrannosaurus Rex who were now enjoying their freedom, not only to roam but, also to kill!

'Here I come!' shouted Cache as he surfed at speed in circles around them.

They snapped at him and on several of his circles he was lucky not be to be caught in their large jaws.

'Take that!' yelled Cache as he swirled around them.

The Tyrannosaurus Rex were only interested in the meals available to them. Since they hadn't had an opportunity such as this before they wanted to enjoy it and Cache firing laser beams at them was becoming a nuisance, a real nuisance.

'Aaarrggghhhh, aaaarrrrggghhh!' cried another Tyrannosaurus Rex as a laser beam bounced off its rear end.

Wonder how close I can get, thought Cache, *maybe if I get right up towards their backs and bounce a couple of shots off them they might panic and run towards the forest for cover.*

'Cache Downloader is the best surfer in town!' he

shouted, smiling.

Cache took off and soon was surfing at around five quantum calamities. He took a curve upwards and, gliding from side to side, he crouched to make himself a smaller target to keep his body out of reach should any large jaws try to take a piece of him. Laser gloves primed he swooped towards the Tyrannosaurus Rex.

Three of them were chasing warthogs that scurried noisily towards the lake, 'Crunch, crackle.' Screams and pig-type whining sounds echoed around as another warthog was caught.

Cache surfed towards them and, being careful not to make too large a target, he fired all his laser beams at the same time in rapid succession.

Cache liked the 'Zzzzzzziiiiiiiipppp' sound of the laser beams as they flew through the air.

'Zzzzziiiiiippppp, zzzziiiiipppp, aaarrrggghhh, aaarrrggggghhh!'

'Zzzziiiiiipppp, zzzziiiiipppppp, zzzzziiiiipppppp, aaarrrgggghhh!'

'Right on the target,' screamed Cache. 'Bottoms sore?' he yelled. 'Wait for the next lot!'

'Zzzzziiiiipppppp, zzzziiiiiipppppp,' flashes flew across the plains as Cache fired more direct hits on the three Tyrannosaurus Rex. Wails of pain filled the air as the three Tyrannosaurus Rex, hurting from the onslaught, began to gallop in the opposite direction and towards the forest.

'Good boys!' cried Cache. 'Now you lot get on your way and I'll deal with the other four.'

Cache concentrated on getting the three Tyrannosaurus Rex safely back into the forest. Reluctantly they moved now at a reasonable speed, with Cache firing intermittently at their rear just to keep them alert and to make sure they didn't try to turn back.

'Weeble, weeble, weeble, we're the Tyrannosaurus Rex, we're the Tyrannosaurus Rex!' called the Bugs as they rumbled across the open plains. Scanner, now armed with a DBM, skirted around the beast. Blast! He let off a single shot and hit the Bug Tyrannosaurus Rex full in the mouth.

'Ouch! Weeble, weeble, weeble,' said the Bug Tyrannosaurus Rex.

Scanner had another go.

Blast!

'Ouch! Weeble, weeble, weeble, what's your game Scanner?' shouted the Bug Tyrannosaurus Rex.

Scanner wanted to have a shot at the rear of the beast, just as Cache had done with the real Tyrannosaurus Rex a few web minutes before. He surfed around and behind, firing warning shots across the belly of the beast.

'Ooohhh hey, hey! Weeble, weeble, weeble!' shouted the Bug Tyrannosaurus Rex in pain. 'Weeble, weeble, weeble, Scanner you watch it!'

Blast!

'Aaaaaoooouuuuuccchhhh! Weeble, weeble, weeble!' cried the Bug Tyrannosaurus Rex in real pain.

Scanner knew he had to work fast to make sure he

eliminated as many Bugs as possible before they had the chance to mould into something different.

Blast!

'Aaaaaoooooouuuuuucccchhhh! Weeble, weeble, weeble!'

As Scanner rounded behind the Bug Tyrannosaurus Rex a thought crossed his mind.

What if I fire at the giant tail, it'll make a good target and will cause maximum discomfort to the Bug Tyrannosaurus Rex and might just flush them all out, he thought.

Scanner surfed in towards the tail, just as he was about to fire off another burst from his DBM, SNAP! The Bug Tyrannosaurus Rex brought its head round swiftly and caught Scanner between its large jaws! Although he was now well and truly trapped and in a little pain, the Bugs couldn't harm Scanner – but they could make his efforts to escape very difficult. They might even take him back to Ram Router's domain as a hostage.

'Cache!' shouted Scanner as he struggled between the jaws of the Bug Tyrannosaurus Rex. 'Hey, you're hurting me!' exclaimed Scanner. 'Just you wait until Cache hears about this, you're history!' he said.

'Weeble, weeble, weeble,' said the Bug Tyrannosaurus Rex. 'Weeble, weeble, weeble, poor little Scanner. Boo hoo hoo! Wait until Cache hears about this,' they smirked. 'Weeble, weeble, weeble. Oh Scanner, what'll you do now?'

Meanwhile Cache had now ushered the three Tyrannosaurus Rex back into the forest compound.

'Right now for the rest,' he said.

He surfed back towards the other four who by now were devouring everything in sight. The small animals were no match for the large and fast Tyrannosaurus Rex. This had been not so much a meal as more of a massacre. Screams of pain and the sounds of wounded animals were everywhere. The open plains resembled a battlefield. Carcasses lay around everywhere.

'What a mess!' exclaimed Cache.

'Zzzzzziiiipppp, zzziiiiiippppp, zzziiiiipppppp.'

'Aarrrgghh, aaarrrrggggghhhh, aaaarrrrggggghhhh, aaaaarrrrgggggghhhh!' as he scored direct hits on all four Tyrannosaurus Rex at the same time.

This laser glove is a smashing invention; the old DBM wouldn't cope with this, thought Cache, *DotCombo and the Surf_Aces will love it. Must find a way of getting DotCombo to endorse it and give me some investment money to make more,* he thought. *It's been field tested in action, what better report could the lovely DotCombo need than this?*

'Zzzzzzzziiiiiippppp, zzzzzzziiiippppp.'

'Aaaaarrrgggghhhh, aaarrrrggghhh!'

'Ha, ha, ha!' called Cache as he surfed in between the Tyrannosaurus Rex firing with both arms outstretched. The beauty of the laser gloves was that you could fire one finger, or two or all of them; it depended on the target.

'Zzzzzziiiippp, zzzzzziiiippppp, zzzzzziiiippppp. Zzzzzziiiipppp, zzzziiipppppp.'

The Tyrannosaurus Rex couldn't cope and started

to run towards the forest.

'On the run at last!' shouted Cache surfing around and behind them and firing from all ten fingers of his laser gloves.

'Help! Cache! Scanner here!'

'Hey Scanner, what's up?' responded Cache.

'The Bug Tyrannosaurus Rex has got me trapped in its jaws. They're heading back towards the exit, I'm a hostage!' he called loudly.

'I need a few more web minutes,' replied Cache. 'They'll not harm you, hold on tight and don't panic.'

Cache quickly rounded on the Tyrannosaurus Rex and let off a couple of shots, one from each of his forefingers just to make sure the four remaining Tyrannosaurus Rex didn't try to turn back or make a run for it, or try to eat him!

They could move at quite some speed, thought Cache as they neared the forest.

Suddenly a couple of Bugs who had been blasted from the earlier probe bounced up and let Cache have it! He was Gloobed! The two Bugs slumped to the ground. It would be 7.3 web minutes before they would be ready to fire again.

'Scanner, I'm Gloobed!' shouted Cache into his Visi-Tel.

'Wow, great, what happens now?' replied Scanner. 'I'm in the jaws of a Bug Tyrannosaurus Rex, heading for Ram Router's domain. I presume, and you're covered in Gloob, some team, eh?' said Scanner.

'The Tyrannosaurus Rex have just gone back into

the forest but we haven't even secured the area yet and they could get back out again,' said Cache.

'DotCombo, come in. Over,' said Cache into his Visi-Tel. 'Scanner and I are in trouble!'

'DotCombo here, over. What's the problem?' she replied.

'We've got the seven Tyrannosaurus Rex back into the forest but they're not secured. I've just been Gloobed and Scanner is trapped in the jaws of a Tyrannosaurus Rex comprised of Bugs!' said Cache.

'Is that all?' said DotCombo dryly. 'I thought you said you had a problem!'

'Hey, DotCombo! This is no laughing matter, we need help!'

'DotCombo, Scanner here. I'm nearly at the exit to the HistoryLand Disk, if the Bugs get me out of here my next call will be Ram Router's domain!' said a worried and frightened Scanner.

'Okay, joke over,' said DotCombo. 'Listen, Icon is on his way to the HistoryLand Disk anyway. I thought you two might need some help just clearing the place up and making it secure. I didn't realise he would need to save your skins and, in your case Scanner, laminated coating as well! Try to hold on, he shouldn't be far,' said DotCombo.

'I can't move!' said Cache, as a group of Bugs who had been scattered began making their way menacingly towards him.

'DotCombo, DotCombo, I'm very scared!' shouted Scanner.

The T-Rex fights back

'Weeble, weeble, weeble, we've got Scanner!' sang the Bug Tyrannosaurus Rex.

'Icon, come in, over!' called DotCombo into her sound accessor.

'Icon here, DotCombo.'

'Are you nearly in the HistoryLand Disk?' she asked.

'Yes, I'm in the new folder we created and I'm just about to surf over to the tracks. I'll be with Cache and Scanner in about 2 web minutes,' he replied.

'Icon, they're both in trouble,' said DotCombo and then explained their predicament.

'Oh great, just great,' said Icon.

'Go fix it, Surf_Ace!' commanded DotCombo. 'And this time make sure there's no mishaps. I want Cache and Scanner out of there pronto, is that clear? Oh, and Icon? Secure the Tyrannosaurus Rex while you're there,' she continued.

'Got it, DotCombo, Icon on his way and ready for action.'

Icon did his customary surfing shuffle, a double back flip, and was off at maybe seven quantum calamities, maybe more!

'Refresh, come in. Over!' called DotCombo.

'Refresh here, DotCombo. Over,' replied Refresh.

DotCombo again explained to Refresh and Media what was happening to Cache and Scanner and that Icon was on his way to help.

'I take it there's nothing happening in the Animal Kingdom Disk?'

'Not a thing,' replied Refresh, 'and Tooltip should be here soon too.'

'I wanted to have a massage and a Jacuzzi in the Health and Beauty Disk,' said Media. 'It's hot and sticky in here, it's like a jungle!'

'It is a jungle,' laughed Refresh.

'Keep me informed of all progress,' said DotCombo.

'Sure will, over,' said Refresh. 'Hey Media,' said Refresh, 'if nothing happens soon, I think old Ram Router might have been bluffing. The real attack may have been in the HistoryLand Disk after all, this has been the decoy.'

'Don't speak too soon,' said Media, 'I can hear weeble, weeble, weeble, sounds coming from the horizon.'

Media was right, millions of Bugs were advancing and the attack on the Animal Kingdom Disk would start any moment now.

'Refresh, the Bugs are here, listen and look,' said Media.

'Keep cool now,' said Refresh. 'We'll go where we can keep sight of the tiger but I don't want them sparked if we can help it, let's keep it tight just for now.'

'Will do, Refresh. Let's see what the Bugs intend to do and then we'll know where we stand,' said Media.

This was the real thing and the Surf_Aces were ready for action.

'DotCombo, come in. Over,' said Refresh. 'The

attack in the Animal Kingdom Disc starts for real any web minute now.'

'Understood, Refresh. You know what you both have to do,' said DotCombo. 'Take care and good luck.'

'We'll need it!' they both exclaimed together.

'Deep breath, Media. Let's go,' said Refresh.

To be continued in book two!

The Sequel

DotCombo, the Surf_Aces and the whole team will return in Book Two as they continue to fight Ram Router and the Bugs.

Ram Router and the Bugs will be creating more mischief, danger, evil schemes and inventions in Book Two!

Plus new stories, adventures and exciting new characters.

DotCombo & the Surf_Aces in Book Two: *Into the Domain*.

See you all there!

Visit DotCombo, the Surf_Aces, Click, Scanner, Cache Downloader and Kydo at their website: www.surf-aces.supanet.com or e-mail them at:: dotcombo@supanet.com; surf-aces@supanet.com

Visit Ram Router and the Bugs at their website: www.ramrouter.supanet.com or e-mail them at: ramrouter@supanet.com thebugs@supanet.com

Visit Bobler at his website: www.bobler.supanet.com or you can e-mail him at: bobler@supanet.com

Printed in the United Kingdom
by Lightning Source UK Ltd.
9533100001B